Riding

Desire

An Anthology of Erotic Writing

Edited by Tee Corinne

BANNED BOOKS
Austin, Texas

PS
509
.L47
R53
1991

Photographs on the back cover by Tee Corinne

A BANNED BOOK

FIRST EDITION
First Printing

Copyright © 1991 by Tee Corinne

Published in the United States of America
By Edward-William Publishing Company
Number 292, P.O. Box 33280, Austin, Texas 78764

All Rights Reserved. No part of this book may be reproduced in any form without written permission from the publisher, except for brief passages included in a review appearing in a newspaper or magazine.

The individual authors in this volume retain control of the rights to their works.

Confessions of a Lesbian Groupie, © 1989 by Carolyn Gage first appeared in *Sinister Wisdom* #38.

ISBN 0-934411-44-1

Library of Congress Cataloging-in-Publication Data

Riding desire : an anthology of erotic writing / edited by Tee Corinne. — 1st ed.
   p. cm.
  ISBN 0-934411-44-1 (alk. paper) : $9.95
  1. Lesbians—Literary collections. 2. Erotic literature, American—Women authors. 3. Women—Sexual behavior—Literary collections. 4. Lesbians' writings, American I. Corinne, Tee, 1943–
PS509.L47R5 1991
810.8′0353—dc20   91-3657
                                                                          CIP

Many people helped bring this book into existence and I am grateful to each and every one. Special thanks go to my partner, Beverly Brown, whose intelligence and skills facilitated all levels of the editorial process. Because of her gardening and cooking I am much healthier as I send this off to the publisher, than I might otherwise have been. Appreciation also goes to Georgia and to Jean Sirius who shared their time and expertise, and to my supportive family of friends.

The photographs on the back cover are arranged alphabetically from left to right. The authors are:

Julie Blackwomon	Maureen Brady	Beth Brant	Tee Corinne	Emma Joy Crone
Terri de la Peña	Natalie Devora	Ayofemi Folayan	Carolyn Gage	Rocky Gámez
Winn Gilmore	Elissa Goldberg	Amanda Hayman	Terri Jewell	Midgett
Mary Morell	Ruth Mountaingrove	Ní Aódagaín	Mona Oikawa	Connie Panzarino
Vickie Sears	Sabrina Sojourner	Christina Springer	Pearl TimesChild	Chea Villanueva
Celeste West				zana

Contents

Introduction v

Mona Oikawa	Stork Cools Wings	1
Celeste West	Proud Mary, Keep On Coming	6
Elissa Goldberg	Wednesday, 7:15 A.M.	14
Beth Brant	Language/Desire	17
Ní Aódagaín	Sometimes	20
Christina Springer	The Haunting	23
Emma Joy Crone	Relax, Enjoy	34
Rocky Gámez	A Matter Of Fact	36
zana	september	44
Julie Blackwomon	Maggie, Sex, And The Baby Jesus, Too ..	47
Connie Panzarino	Kaicha	54
Terri Jewell	The Comet Watchers	57
Maureen Brady	excerpt from *Rocking Bone Hollow*	61
Tee Corinne	Invisible Lines	73
Amanda Hayman	Across The Straits Of Georgia	75
Natalie Devora	White Chocolate	83
Chea Villanueva	Friends	88
Midgett	Brown Mommy	93
Vickie Sears	Baskets and Rugs	97
Sabrina Sojourner	Letter Home	114
Pearl Times'sChild	One August	116
Ayofemi Folayan	Texas Two-Step	123
Carolyn Gage	Confessions of a Lesbian Groupie	129
Mary Morell	Tomorrow Morning	136
Ruth Mountaingrove	The Chemistry Between Us	139
Winn Gilmore	The Dinner Guest	144
Terri de la Peña	Blue	149

Contributors notes 155

Introduction

In the process of editing *Riding Desire*, my second anthology of erotic writing, I began asking myself questions about the intellectual structures within which I was working. What was I trying to accomplish in this gathering of stories? What kinds of choices was I making around who to invite, length of story, style? Where, indeed, did my sense of what made a story come from?

I realized that I was imagining the stories as if they were being told around a table after dinner, or around a campfire — both images come out of the Southern story telling traditions with which I grew up. Mine was not a literary family, but we listened to and told stories — some real and some fanciful — and listened to the radio. Television did not, at first, exist, and when it did arrive, it was not very important in my life.

So I understand this book as a gathering of voices telling stories which I hope will resonate in the lives of readers, and, as in the tradition in which I grew up, each story takes as long as it needs. I am a minimal editor, wanting stories to be understandable, yet not wanting to pull them tightly into a single format or tight grammatical mold. Part of what makes them so interesting for me lies in their structural differences as well as in the stories told.

Often, as a reader, I will start a book with the contributors' notes as a way to become acquainted with the authors themselves before I sample their writings. In *Riding Desire* as in *Intricate Passions*, I encouraged authors to give detailed biographical statements. The contributors notes thus become a series of brief stories, distillations of many different lives.

As a "grassroots" intellectual, a person who loves ideas, I wanted to deepen the current discourse on sexuality. I invited the authors to write about their interest in erotic/sex writing and what they wanted to accomplish in the process of telling their stories.

Because I was a child in a violent household, a child who was molested, I cared to make this an anthology which was safe for me to edit, for you to read. I looked for stories about how sexuality could work with the bodies we have, within our disparate personal histories. And sometimes a story which was pure fantasy would catch me and spin me away.

In general I invited authors who had already published sexual/sensual stories. I wanted to honor people who were willing to risk writing sex when it wasn't as popular as is currently the case. I was also looking for stories the likes of which I hadn't heard before.

So gather near for a series of intimate tales and visceral confabulations. The pleasure of your company is warmly appreciated.

Tee A. Corinne
Southern Oregon
March, 1991

Stork Cools Wings

Mona Oikawa

I met Lisa in my Tai Chi class. We were the only two Asian women in a room full of tall white men. Our one consolation about this setting was that from the moment we saw each other we had knotted a bond of sisterhood, tight as the clasps formed by our hands in the mirrored movements we practice in our strengthening exercises. We had quickly discovered we are both third generation Canadians: she is of Chinese origin, I am of Japanese descent.

A few days ago, I went to Lisa's house for tea. The conversation turned, as it always does between us, to being Asian women in a racist society. By the light of candles and burning incense, we talked about our own racism. We compared the stereotypes fed to us by our parents about each other's cultures—she in bowls filled with long and separate grains of rice, me in short-grained sticky servings. We both cried when we talked about how we had internalized racism toward other Asian peoples and now knew it was a reflection of our anger turned inward, the scars of self-hate and self-denial. Before I finally left at one a.m., we had hugged long and hard. I had not wanted to leave.

Week after week I watch Lisa grow stronger, thighs spreading through *tor yus* and *don yus*. My favorite moment is seeing her hands flutter earth and skyward through stork cools wings, beautiful hands poised in mid-flight. When she carries tiger to the mountain, I, too, leave the earth transported by a secret vision of her firm brown body flying and alighting on me, lifting me to sheltered summits rising in mist above my bed. This image has burned deep into my source of yearning, and keeps me restless, night upon sleepless night.

"The class is starting," Lisa whispers, gently pulling my hand. "Are you okay?"

"I'm fine," I answer with an embarrassed grin. "I really have to watch your movements closely. I'm having trouble with my brush knees."

Lisa hurries to take her special sunlit spot. "Let's practice them then. Meet me at the Sun Yat-Sen statue tomorrow at 2 p.m."

The next day, the sky glowed fresh from a morning rain. We had completed one set, hands and legs in perfect harmony, two Asian women, stroking and striding together.

"Your brush knees look better." Lisa states, weaving her long black rivers of hair into soft entwining coils. "I think it's a good idea for us to practice together . . . Not to change the subject, but I just read your story on Asian lesbians and safer sex. Do you really use Saran Wrap?"

Nearly choking on the tea I am sipping from my thermos, I wonder why she is asking me this question. I knew she had ended her relationship with a man over a year ago, but despite my daily fantasizing, I assumed she was still very straight.

"I'm really not an expert on safer sex. I actually have never used Saran Wrap. In fact, the latest research indicates that plastic wrap may not be an effective barrier against the HIV virus, so I wouldn't recommend it." I'm trying to hide my insecurity, I think to myself, as I hear the familiar academic-trained voice come from somewhere inside me.

"It's all pretty scary to me." Lisa says, her dark brown eyes piercing my veil of confidence. "What do you use then?"

The truth is I hadn't been able to make love to a woman since I had met her six months ago. "We can talk about it over dinner, if you wish. Want to come back to my place?"

"How long have you been into macrobiotics?" Lisa asks, tasting the azuki beans I'd cooked in garlic and ginger.

"I took a course over a year ago. But actually, these foods are a part of my history. I guess I'm trying to reclaim them."

"That's how I feel about Tai Chi." Lisa's hands are beating the air to illustrate her point. "But I get angry when I feel I'm depending on white people, like our teacher, to help us learn our histories."

As we pass the teapot between us, Lisa reminds me about continuing our safer sex discussion. "Can I see a dental dam?" She smiles with the warm openness I have come to cherish. "I assume you have a ready supply of them."

"I do have a few somewhere." I am shaking with nervousness and excitement. I go into the bedroom and open the creaking drawer of the dresser my grandmother gave me. I reach for the box of bubble-gum flavour and carry it to this beautiful woman with hand outstretched.

"How do you use them?" she asks very seriously. Now, I am confused. Does she really want a demonstration?

I tell her matter-of-factly, how lube can be applied to the side covering the skin, and how either partner can hold it in place. I don't elaborate with descriptions of the leather straps I've seen for allowing hands their wandering freedom, or the garter belts like the black lace one that sits unused in that same creaky drawer.

"I really think I should be tested for HIV," Lisa says quietly. "My ex and I were non-monogamous and I never asked him to wear a condom with me. I haven't been with anyone else since we broke up, but I know I have to practice safer sex. I don't want to put myself or anyone else at risk. But I'm scared of being tested. And scared of not knowing what to do when I want to sleep with someone."

My eyes do not leave her face as I admit, "I'm afraid too. I've thought of being tested. Even though I was monogamous in my last relationship, I did have unprotected sex with my lover, and a lot of women before her. I've decided it's best for me to practice safer sex. I feel it's an issue of respect and not differentiating between certain types of lovers — making categories of safe and unsafe people. It's some of our practices and not protecting ourselves that may be unsafe . . . But I do miss being able to do some things without barriers."

"Maybe we could go to the clinic and get tested together," Lisa says, taking my hand in hers. I feel her pulse with the tips of my fingers. Is it racing as fast as mine?

"I have to think more about it. But I'd be happy to go with you if you decide to take the test."

"It's late. The subway has stopped running," Lisa yawns. "Can I stay here tonight?"

"We'll both have to sleep on the pull-out couch. I still haven't finished my loft." I am trying to calm my voice by clearing the teacups and picking up crumbs from the table.

"That's fine." She is rummaging through the cabinet in the bathroom. "Do you have an extra toothbrush?"

I put the dental dams back in their hiding place. I try to stop thinking of how I would like to use every one of the thirty-six dams in the box with the woman who will share my bed tonight. I am flushed from the sight of her holding the six by six inch piece of latex between her incredibly beautiful hands.

I really must stop fantasizing, I tell myself, crawling into bed beside her. I must not turn or my face will be a breath away from her back.

She, however, is not as careful in this bed made for one and a half women. Her hand is on my hip now and I try to move away. She must be asleep, I chant silently, my heart beating up through my throat into my mouth.

But her hand is moving toward my breast and I am wanting her, hoping her fingers will rise to fondle my nipples, erupting at the feel of her.

"Where are the dental dams?" Lisa whispers softly in my ear.

"In the bottom drawer of the dresser," my voice is barely audible.

She scrambles away from me and I know she has found the other box in my latex stash.

"What do we do with the gloves?" she shouts.

"They are used for penetration," I reply.

"We will need them then," she says, lighting a candle and placing it by the bed.

I reach for her. Our mouths join, our tongues search first tentatively, then lustfully. She is on top of me now. Rubbing the inside of my thigh with her knee, she moans, "This is how I do brush knee." I grasp her knee hard between my legs, while she lifts my t-shirt and begins to lick in circles around my breasts. I take her beautiful hands in mine, raise them to my lips, and pull each finger deep into my mouth, one by one.

I move her beneath me and begin to travel the paths of our foremothers, through crevice and moss, uncovering treasures with mouth and hand. When I reach the hollow of her navel, she pleads, "I want to go down on you first."

"You're very butch for a woman who's just coming out," I tease.

"I know you haven't thought of me as a lesbian, but I have wanted you ever since I saw you do your first Tai Chi set." She is hovering above me and I am captive of the sight. "And that night you came to my house, I didn't want you to leave."

Lisa is going down my body with her tongue. In leaps and bounds, she is stirring within me feelings of joy and hope and love. She slides a lilac-colored dam over my wetness and says, "You are dark like me, so dark, so beautiful." She begins to lick me slowly, then with urgency. I am entering that other plane of consciousness, panting in rhythm with each of her mouthfuls of me.

She stops suddenly. "What's wrong?" I ask. She is sitting upright, "I don't care for the taste of bubble-gum and rubber. I want to taste you."

"We can rinse the dam, it helps . . . And there's a little bottle in my fridge door with a drawing of a Japanese woman on it. Get it," I urge frantically. It seems she is gone forever. Unscrewing the bottle cap, she returns.

"What is it?"

The tension is subsiding between my legs. "It's ume paste. Smear it on your side of the dental dam."

"It looks like dried blood," she says.

"That's why I like it." I answer, adding, "It's actually dried plums, very macrobiotic." She laughs and I feel a cold sensation as she spoons out the thick red paste while the dam is still on me. I will not need any lube tonight.

Her tongue is licking upward and around. She eats the ume noisily. "It is salty. Your blood is delicious." I rise and come quickly beneath her.

We wait long moments, hands clasped tightly, brown skin breathing on brown skin.

"I really think it's time for you to practice your brush knees." Lisa smiles, her lips showing spots of ume red. "But please use this for my dental dam." She pulls my black lace garter belt from the green and white box, over her legs, and up her powerful thighs. "There are lots of things we could use, you know," she says, passing me the bottle of ume.

"Like what?" I ask, pulling her face into mine.

"Come to my house tomorrow and I'll show you."

I climb Lisa's soft brown body, my wings circling her head. Her delicate hands flutter through my hair and around me joyfully. Incense wisps of jasmine and cherry blossom rise in clouds above our bed. 'Til the light of dawn, we carry each other to the peaks of Tian Shan and Fuji-san. Arms and legs in perfect harmony, two Asian women stroking and striding and flying together.

---

note: Technically it is umeboshi paste. Ume means plum. Umeboshi is pickled plum.

Proud Mary, Keep On Coming

Celeste West

My uptown darling Anne ("with an 'E' ") was impressed that first morning after the night before. I had rolled out of bed onto her inch deep "dusky rose" carpet to do my usual hundred push-ups. Then I did thirty-five more because I was feeling like hot stuff, plus I am a double Leo and a show-off.

"Well, Sailor," she asked, "did the Navy teach you exercises for that great tongue muscle, too?"

"Yes, ma'am," I said. "I am the only dyke sailor who can push a bowling ball up spiral stairs."

"Come here," she said, opening the quilt and her beautiful legs. I did. I showed her what an old sailor with a physically fit tongue can do when the tide is high. I tasted the salt spray in my face again and the wild tang and swell of the ninth ninth wave as she begins to gather. When I went for Anne's breasts, the nipples were so taut that I was sure she would come all over me when I rolled and kneaded them. "Harder," she commanded, so I changed tack and drove into each of her two hot holes with my fingers and thumb as I nibbled and sucked those breasts. She shuddered, screaming such a torrent as would make a sailor blush . . . Then quick, it was all cool-down, up-town because Anne, despite the 'E', was not to be late to the seven-name office where she was a lawyer.

"You're new here, Sailor," she said, carefully fastening the snaps on her black garter belt, smoothing her hands down her thigh just to sex me up again.

"Yes," I said, "but I am bold and gay and gallant and I aim to please." I ran my fingers slowly around her stocking top. When I got in to stroke some thigh, she rolled her pussy at me, then her eyes. I made an important mental note that there were violets in those deep blue eyes. I made another important mental note on how Anne would look in crotchless panties. I could get a pair for her to wear under those garters. Then I would meet her for lunch at some quiet little place with booths and long white table cloths.

"No, I mean you're new to town, Sailor," she said impatiently. "Came to retire in San Francisco, that's hilarious. I'm in a blood battle to become a lowly associate by the time I'm forty-five — if I'm lucky — and you're already retired at forty-five! No wonder you stuck with the goddamn military pushing bowling balls."

"Someone had to do it."

"Yeah, and you'd better come around here pretty often to keep that tongue in shape." She gave me a big open-mouth kiss and a couple of great thrusts from garterland.

"I don't mind if I do," I said, putting my pantsleg between her smooth stockinged thighs. I looked into the violets again, feeling I was going to swoon on deck.

"Besides," she said, caressing my belly and crotch, "you're tending toward a little abdominal prolapse, so I think I'll just give you a membership in my women's exercise club, a sort of welcome to the San Francisco dyke tone."

"Wham-bam, thank you, Anne."

"Don't be cute, Sailor. You've still got a fabulous body, but we mid-life women don't have to balloon like Humpty-Dumpties or crumble to osteoporosis. No, thank you."

"Yes, thank you, I accept," I said because all I could deal with was the blood rushing to my cheeks and the sweat pouring down my sides. Anne's hair was surrounded with pulsing silvery light like the halos they painted on saints in the olden days. Whenever I get this blinding kind of hot flash, I take to thinking of angels. I sometimes pretend I'm being "washed in the blood of the lamb," as my grandmother used to say. It is better to feel religious than crazy.

"Whatever is the matter?" Anne demanded. Now her eyelashes were like spun silver with the violet pools calling me deeper. I forgot where here was. All I could repeat was "yes, yes, yes."

"Well, great," said Anne briskly. "I can meet you at the Club on Mondays and Fridays after the office. We can work out and dine on 'lite cuisine' at the Club's restaurant. Then we can come home and fuck the lights on."

Oh, Anne, the lights are already on, you are drenched in glory. I can see your shining, original face, and you are not a lawyer at all. There are roses between your legs. You are like a picture I saw long ago of Saint Joan of Arc. There are banners flying, and I am flying, flying, flying into your eyes.

"Sailor, you're so flushed! Oh, my god, are you flashing?"

"I . . . am in menomorphosis . . ." I explained, making a word salad like I sometimes do.

"Menopause, you mean," Anne said. "Now, I'll be delighted when the last egg rolls down. Then, of course, I'll do estrogen replacement. We mid-life women don't have to take it lying down."

Lie down on me Anne, cover me with all your silvered satin and dusky rose as our mounds blossom with the ancient power.

"Right again," I said aloud, as the colored satin banners of all the galaxies were flying.

* * *

After the gym thing later that evening, Anne got me a "garden apartment" the very next day. Garden apartments are what they call rented cellars in San Francisco, like what I thought at the gym was satin was Spandex. My place is pretty tony though with light coming out of the walls in scallop shells known as "sconces." I wouldn't mind more windows, but for awhile I lived on a sub, so what the hell. Besides, Lady Anne also called the place her "love nest." She was right again there. Like most women into heavy vanilla, she liked a lot of it, only she called it "high concept" sex. You mainly have to remember to light the candles.

Then I wanted a cat to go with the teensy garden in back. Sure enough, a stray came calling. He had six toes on one of his paws, like I have an extra toe on one foot myself. An ear was half gone. That tom and me had a few lives in common, so I invited him to stay. Anne was furious. She said he was yang energy and how could I stand it? When she explained to me the whole yin/yang theory of reverse polarity, I thought: right again.

So I went to the SPCA and got a marmalade-colored female kitten to balance the yang energy in the garden apartment. I also got a tattoo on the left cheek of my ass showing the yin/yang commas at play in their cosmic dance. It is the same black and red colors I had once seen as an emblem on railroad freight cars before I knew the deep meaning of that image. Anne was unusually pleased with the tattoo, if not with Senior Six-Toes and Marmalade Me. She started paying more attention to my buns, and life was real hot and rosy again.

Then, without us realizing it, Marmalade Me passed swiftly and secretly from kitten to child bride. In the part of the closet I reserved for Lady Anne, Marmalade Me had five kittens, all yang and all with six toes. They were born in Anne's cashmere skirt. She blew up. Anne hated being in the same house with kitty litter and she hated orange hair on her suits, not to mention bolts of yang energy jumping on her head at night. She said, "It is either the goddamn cats or me."

"What do you want me to do, drown them in the toilet or pop them in the mailbox for early delivery?" I asked. "Why don't we just make love in your flat, what with its breakneck view and that fireplace and all?"

So that's what we did. I got Marmalade Me fixed along with all her yang six-toed. I bought a good lint brush for my dates with Lady Anne, having learned on shipboard the fine art of compromise. Senior Six-Toes seemed to stroke his long whiskers and smile whenever I went off to Lady Anne's. Then he usually gave me a physical fitness demo like a show-off yogi, since he has twenty-six more vertebrae than any mere human being. Our main exercise, besides my regular push-ups of course, was sexercise, as Lady Anne called it. Her clit could get so big, I gave it its own zip code number. The gym dates, unfortunately, had petered out because Anne got busy with becoming an associate most evenings as well as days. I took to walking alone on the piers and the beach. I was thinking of getting a dog to go with me.

Then I myself had to take a job appraising houses a few times a week. This is because I virtually hot-flashed me out of the Navy Reserve and probably lost my Navy income. After all these years, push came to shove, with them butch-baiting me for the last time. I flashed like blue lightning, shouted that damn right I was queer. "Queer as a six-toed cat!" I yelled, after a lot of mealy-mouth questions from a prick Lieutenant. Anne was furious at me for blowing it, but got me lawyers who specialize in these cases. The lawyers seemed pretty shaken up themselves because at the time I came out to the Navy I also mooned my yin/yang tattoo right at the Lieutenant, and everyone cheered. So it's probably a wash-out, though the lawyers are costing me a fortune. I suspect it all goes up their noses.

Anne really cooled out after the suit's publicity. She said she was terribly sorry, but I could be a liability to her career, guilt by association and all. Right again, I suppose. A woman's gotta do what a woman's gotta do. I don't blame her; I hid out over twenty years. Sometimes I have dreams of Anne as a splendid figurehead on an olden days clippership, breasts like the hemispheres of heaven. She sails by and I wave. I still do thirty-five extra push-ups for her. Senior Six-Toes yawns. Cats have real muscles in their backs instead of ligaments like people, so they don't break as easy as we do.

* * *

I decided to go back to the gym just to keep up with the cats. If I could jump ten times my height from a standing position, would Lady Anne drop her Spandex? Actually, today I feel myself beginning to come out of the Lady Anne Slump. Women come and go, mainly they come. Still, when I arrive at the gym, I see a woman on the hip abduction machine with blood-red fingernails, same polish as Anne's. I get goose bumps and hot flash like chrome in the sun. In the locker room, I scope out the territory. Nice asses raise my clit at least half-mast. "Maybe there'll be an ice-break this spring," I pray. "Oh, my heart."

"What's that you say, Sailor?"

"Do you know exercises for a broken heart?" I ask, anything to keep the conversation going. Anything. I am now looking at the hottest number I've seen since Tina Turner. This one is not in Club Spandex, so I can't see her nipples, but I can almost feel them salute me. Just a fantasy? Is she even a dyke? She has long tawny hair which would look great on my pillow. No tattoos that I can see and no ring on her fuck finger. But she has that little swagger as she comes nearer, and there's the half-smile.

"Aerobics and fucking," she says real sweet and sincere like.

"What?"

"For the heart. Ride the exercycle or a wild filly at least thirty minutes a day. Your heart will swing open one more time."

"Is that a promise?" I ask, all ruffled.

"It's no lie," she says. "Keep me posted." Then she goddamn winks.

"Do you have a card?" I ask, like the corporate ladies do to get a phone number.

"Here's a prescription for you I found in the laundromat," she says. Then she takes a bar of soap and writes huge on the double mirror:

Unstiffen your supple body.
Unchatter your quiet mind.
Unfreeze your fiery heart.

"Hey, you can't WRITE on mirrors!" shouts some self-appointed Sergeant-at-arms.

"The hell I can't," she says, striding off to the stair machine like some Proud Mary.

I ride that damn exercycle for thirty minutes, pumping imaginary bellows to create heat that will unfreeze my fiery heart. I am also working up the nerve to ask Proud Mary out for coffee or something. I go to the hall to get a drink, but when I get back to the gym, damned if she hasn't disappeared. So has her prescription on the mirror; old Sarge no doubt. Well, I blew it, but what a feeling! What a prescription to tell the kittencaboodle waiting for me back at the garden apartment.

I begin showering with a little whistle, the first real song since Lady Anne. Then, Mamasita!, who should come in the shower room? Proud Mary's hair is now swept up in one of those French rolls of yesteryear, but looser. Her pussy is a darker color than her hair, more bronze. I have to remember to breathe because her body takes my breath away. That "Rose of Sharon" phrase from the Bible somehow comes to me. I never realized what it meant before. Our Lady of the Blazing Roses, open to me.

"I thought you'd gone," I manage to say.

"I was hoping you'd join me in the sauna," she says.

I can just stare like a jerk. "Is that why you're so rosy?"

"Oh, I'm rosy all right." Her eyes graze my body until my face is as rosy as she is.

"Now one thing I really admire is an ass with a philosophical turn," she says, as I move, hot and shy, toward my shower.

"Are you a Taoist?" she asks pleasantly.

I look pretty dumb. "What is a Taoist?"

"Well, if you don't know, you just may be one," she says, turning on her shower. "Anyway, you have a sweet Buddha belly and a Taoist ass."

"I am a fisher of women," I say for absolutely no reason whatsoever. Then I cover that by saying, "I am a sailor," when I am probably not even in the Reserves anymore, but what the hell.

"Good," she smiles, "Then you have seen the world."

While I wonder if she is being sarcastic or what, she says, "Sailor, there's no soap in my shower dispenser. Do you have some in yours?"

I squeeze my hand full of pearly suds and offer them to her.

"Soap me," she says softly. Oh, Proud Mary. I start with her wings because this seems proper at first, then her beautiful neck and full back. When I get to her ass, the soap is lathering up like spindrift on a wild beach, so of course I spend quite awhile on this landscape. Then I lather her long legs. I am on my knees, and she is now leaning with both hands against the colored tiles. She is breathing hard and begins saying things that make the water steam.

She moans and turns. I rise up to soap the breasts of a queen. When I go down both her arms, our fingers slip together like two starfish. I can almost feel the valleys of our fingerprints. I fully believe mine can grow little starfish suction cups as I massage under her arms into her curling armpit hair. She moans deeper now, and tongue kisses me so good I can feel it all the way to my sixth toe.

Contrary to twenty years of Navy training, I have left my shower blasting. It is steaming up the room, but not enough. There are just the shower heads against the wall, no stalls, so if someone comes in, they will see me lathering one real sexed-up woman almost to fucking orgasm. I am a bitch in heat myself. I know I have to get in and fuck her, but what if someone like that damned Sergeant stumbles in? I'll be kicked out of the gym like I was the Reserves.

So be it: I'll work out in hell. I laugh as I plow through beautiful dripping pussy hair. I squeeze her swollen outer lips. She whispers into my ear, "Dive into it, Sailor. Dive into it. Dive in it and I'll suck yours to glory."

A deal's a deal with a Proud Mary. I push her against the wall, spreading her inner lips with one hand while I push two fingers good and deep into port. She grabs my body to her as I play the tip of her clit like a bluegrass fiddle. She gasps, then lurches so that I am practically holding her up. Biceps, triceps and deltoids don't fail me now, I pray, as she whips me up to push more and more sweet pleasure into her body.

The water steams around us. She finally relaxes in my arms, smiles into my very cells and says, "I want your ass and phone number, Sailor."

"I'll write the number on the mirror," I say, noticing that the soap dispenser next to her shower was full all along.

"How's your heart?" she asks.

"It's beating real hard."

"Happy heart on," she says. She cups her hand over my chest and then smooths her fingers round my breast. She squeezes it good, bends down to suck the nipple, and starts licking water off my body.

"I'm going to breast-fuck you," she says, "then you are going to let me open up the cleavage of that hard little sailor's ass."

My nipples are getting hot and holy under her lips. I am almost there when, wham — oh, the old silver light begins bathing the mist like we've opened the Pearly Gates. Light ricochets rainbows in the steam. As she penetrates me, blue streaks seem to shoot from her fingers. Passion falls on me in veils of mist. I gather up its sheerest folds of silken light and press them to me again and again.

"I must be hot flashing."

"Ah."

I sink to the floor with the rivers of light in the water coursing across the tiles. Proud Mary cradles me in her arms, and I know when I come that I was never empty of love. My lover whispers things to me from oceanic time which I didn't know that I knew — about being at sea and in harbor as one swirling yin/yang, about Love, the Great Skyrider.

Suddenly, someone stands over us.

"She's hot flashing. It's okay."

"Oh, my gawd," says the Sergeant from above.

"We'll be fine," my lover says.

"It's from going in that sauna, I'll just bet," says the Sergeant.

"Right again," I whisper.

"You'd better stay out of that sauna when you're here."

"You'd better stay off our planet," says my lover. Sarge stomps off.

I laugh in Proud Mary's lap, and she kisses on me.

"I guess I'll take a cool shower," I say, finally standing up.

"You just do that," Proud Mary says, licking into my wet pussy like a woman who can push a mean bowling ball herself. She slaps my yin/yang and heads for the lockers. I am still under the shower when she strides in like a lightfoot buckeroo, fully dressed. Her cowboy boots echo on the tiles.

"I got dressed only so you could come over and undress me sometime," she says. "Real easy, like this," as she opens my pussy very slowly. She has tightly rolled her business card. She sucks it like a joint and pushes it into my cunt gently, but with a little twist so I feel it go up there all right. She puts her hand on my heart. "Make a special nook for me." Then she actually clicks her heels three times, and, like Dorothy, is gone.

I float into the locker room and see old Sarge. With a crisp nod, she says, "That woman drives me crazy every time she comes."

Pressing out a business card very wet from the high seas, I say, "Right again."

Wednesday, 7:15 A.M.

Elissa Goldberg

It was the only seat left on the bus, third space back from the driver. Emma knew it was the only seat left. She knew it without scanning the length of the bus. She knew it by the woman's eyes, space number two. Dark hazel-green eyes that held Emma, swallowed her, then without a word nor pause, explained: "This is it. This is all there is."

Emma reached for the pole, then twisted around and sat down, squeezing herself between two legs, two shoulders, a tight space. It was a cold morning and she had too many things. She lifted her purse, her gym bag, a paper lunch sack onto her lap, settled her umbrella against her knee, then folded the newspaper across the top of the pile. She felt like she was carrying loads of potatoes down to market. She felt like her grandmother. She felt on display, as one set of dark hazel eyes detailed her features: eyelashes, nose, lips, chin. Emma knew her skin was reddening, could remember the combed ridges in her still wet hair, the puffy bags beneath her eyes. She stared straight ahead, her shoulders rigid. Soon it would be her turn. Emma reached across the newspaper and, holding her packages, shifted her weight back against the seat, then carefully removed the Living section from its folded order and placed it on top.

From her left, Emma could feel another pair of eyes stare at the columns, dance next to her own gaze down the length of the page. Without shifting her head, Emma looked at her neighbor's lap. A full-length, black wool coat, two ungloved hands. The woman's fingers were long and neatly manicured. Strong and graceful hands, Emma knew their carefulness, could sense their deliberate slowness in opening envelopes or packages, turning the pages of a book.

Emma focused back to the paper, and again felt the woman's eyes on her neck. Her chest tightened. It wasn't the first time this had happened. People had been staring at her often these past few weeks, drawn to her, as if they knew the twists and turns her body was making, as if they could smell Connie's scent on her fingers, in her hair. She, herself, was constantly being reminded. The morning meeting, and she'd reach to her cheek and smell sex. A phone call, and her mind would wander to the night before, to her tongue and fingers teasing the buttons of Connie's Levis. Thinking about it brought soft pushing sounds from her throat. Emma glanced up at the other passengers. All the faces pale, shut down. She turned back to the page in front of her.

Sometimes she liked the sense of power she felt when people watched her. She felt in control, even daring, as she opened connections with people, like windows, then shut them when she was ready to leave. Walking down the street she'd swing her hips loudly, smile to feel the bounce of her breasts. It had been a long time. She felt warm and alive and hungry, and her hunger only grew and grew.

But it was a dangerous hunger, too. She feared it leaked through her work clothes, pulled at her composure during staff meetings, board meetings, conversations with her boss. She felt scared at times, trapped like a steeped teabag, hot, and undeniably stained.

Emma opened and folded the paper over. Her neighbor's head turned to stare at the horoscope. Wonder what she is, Emma thought. Taurus, Virgo? She knew nothing about star signs, listened half-heartedly when the subject came up at parties. Maybe this woman is one of those Believers, she thought. A wild woman, she'd love Emma for hours, barely lift her mouth for a breath, then push onto her elbows to announce Emma's attributes as a Pisces with a moon in Cancer. Emma clenched her knees to keep from laughing. She stared at Ann Landers, then felt too exposed and creased the paper back to its original position.

Emma and Connie had been lovers for only a month, but friends for years. It wasn't an easy transition, peeling away layers of clothing, familiarity, expectations. But it was exciting. Each meeting, pressing ideas into skin, into mouths. Talking and twisting, soaking, they learned new doors, new curved paths. Sometimes, pushing away from each other in bed, each heart slowly quieting in a separate chest, they stared into changed eyes, old and familiar, and completely foreign.

Emma shook the paper. She strained her eyes to the black and white. Her neighbor bent a smooth neck around Emma's shoulder. She was silent, waiting, steady. She's a cat, Emma thought. She has night vision, can see apparitions, ghosts dance and travel about the room. She'd move stealthily, plan each placement of her hand. When she was warm, she'd arch her back and demand to be rubbed.

The bus came to a sudden stop, and Emma felt her belongings slip from her knees. She reached to hold them, crushing the newspaper, and felt an arm reaching also to steady her. She looked into dark hazel pools, dimpled cheeks. The woman did not smile as she pushed Emma's bags back onto her lap. But she wasn't unfriendly. She held Emma's gaze calmly, her breathing slow and even. Emma stared at her, could feel her jaw slacken, her lips held apart. She knew the bus was on the bridge, crossing the river, knew they'd soon be downtown. But she and this woman were at the bottom of the river, their bodies poised, muscles taut. In blue-green waters, Emma felt her throat open. Her breath was long and sinewy. They faced each other, their eyes searching for rocks and soft shells. Emma's tongue brushed her own dry lips. She felt two fingers carefully, tentatively touch her jacket, open it. One snap, then two. The fingers pulled at a shirt button, traced its roundness, then slipped it from its hole. Two fingers became three, became four, until one whole hand curved itself around her breast, warmed her nipple.

Emma's tongue was full against her bottom teeth. Her breathing was light and quick. She closed her mouth. They were downtown, the bus two blocks from Emma's stop. Around her, passengers were rising, pulling hats and scarves back into place. She brought her bags against her chest. She had a long day in front of her. The bus drew to a stop and Emma placed her feet on the rubber mat. She clasped her arms around her bags, tucked the newspaper under one arm, then rose to her feet. One black overcoat rose next to her. Emma saw the ungloved hands, then felt her own arms loosen, and turned to watch her purse and gym bag fold to the floor, the newspaper slide into six separate sections. An orange from her lunch sack rolled and knocked against street boots and shoes, curved down the early morning aisle.

Language/Desire
for Denise

Beth Brant

"Will you accept a collect call from Beth Brant?"
The beloved voice says, "Yes, of course."
And a pierce, a tremor, an earthquake moves my body
from this place to yours.
I touch the telephone cord as if to feel
you moving along the wires.
I am home-sick for you. I am body-sick for you.
I am longing.
There is a place in me that needs to touch that out-flung arm
and trace the curve of it starting with the long fingers,
the sweet roundness of the arm itself,
the hollow place where arm and torso meet,
the silk-like hairs growing from under the arm that I
stroke and kiss and lick — the taste of your flesh
filling my mouth with desire.
Desire.
I desire that hollow place.
Here, 3,000 miles away I bathe and when I bathe
the cloth follows the curves and skin of myself and I am
following you.
Lovers.
Here, 3,000 miles away from you
I dream of violent things.
I dream of violence happening.
Your body is not next to mine to keep the nightmares
a step behind.
I can't turn and feel my breast touching your back.
I can't turn and feel your breast in my hand.
That breast.

That breast—large—filling my hand with desire.
That breast.
It speaks in my hand.
My fingers feel a language on that breast.
A language we've invented between ourselves.
This is the language of desire.
Underneath that breast—the salty taste of sweat.
My tongue leaving its imprint on your taste.
My hands following you again.
The beautiful waist that follows its course from rib
to voluptuous hip.
The skin.
The flesh.
My mouth makes a circuit around your waist, your hip.
I make my mark on your body with my tongue.
The legs.
The limbs.
Sturdy. Solid.
The muscle in the calves clenching and letting go.
Clenching and loosening beneath my finger tips.
The language of your legs traveling along my hand.
This is the language between two women.
My own leg feeling the touch of my hand as I touch you.
The thighs.
The thighs.
The secret birthmark on the inside of the right thigh
that is shaped like a star.
I touch the mark with my fingers.
Tracing the shape until it is indelible on my skin.
My mouth feeling the shape take root in my body.
Somewhere in my body I feel it take root and desire
is the language between two women.
The thighs moving and sighing beneath my tongue.
The language.
Your thighs opening and calling my name.
I open you.
You open to me—to my imprint.
The scent of openness making signs on my fingers.
The trails of wet language coating my hand.
The scent.
The scent. The language.

The words enter my mouth.
The folds of skin are speaking on my tongue.
The clitoris is swelling.
The swelling clitoris.
It gives. It moves and
language is the desire between two women.
My tongue tasting the liquid.
Swallowing the scent.
Hearing the openness of your speech.
The liquid seeping its words onto me.
Into me.
This language.
These words.
This speech between two women.

Sometimes

Ní Aódagaín

It's difficult sometimes . . . being her lover . . . not because she isn't a devoted or skillful one. Oh, to the contrary. Hands that wield a garden fork or shovel with prowess, a hammer or saw with strength and stamina, these same hands touch me and stroke me with the gentleness of a butterfly's wings. Lighting here, there, caressing me with oh, such lovely care and attention, she can bring pleasure to every part of myself.

No, it isn't that she doesn't know how to love me, nor that she doesn't want to. Rather it is that she can't. She can't because she is an incest survivor. She lives with memories of touching that turned into hurting, that turned into violence against her; so that now, as she uncovers those deeply buried wounds both in her body and of her spirit, she sometimes can't touch, or be touched.

For, in response to her touching of me, I reach out to touch her. Yet, that touching, my touching her, my lips on her neck, my hand stroking her buttocks, my body on top of her; those intimate moments of loving shared by two wimmin have the power to warp time and reality. So, in response to my touch, she, my lover can return to the past and experience those events of horror again. And so, sometimes, in fact many times, our lovemaking is stopped midway or never begun.

Thus, as her lover, I have felt my caresses go "unnoticed," my first exploring strokes of her breasts be met with stiffness. I recognize that her body is saying "no." So, what do I do? What of the fire that sparks when, from across a room, I am moved by the wholeness of her beauty? What of the passion that grows inside me as I lie in her arms before going to sleep? What of my wanting of her?

Oh, yes, what of my wanting of her? I love this womon deeply. Sometimes my body aches with the desire to suckle her breast, to stroke her firm belly, to lick the warm wetness between her thighs, to speak this most sacred language of love to her. What do I do because I understand that, sometimes, this language is for her a language of torture . . . and I respect her refusal to journey to that place of potential pain?

Sometimes, I turn to myself.

I don't go there often. For making love to myself brings a different pleasure than when she and I make love together. Rather, I have practiced being present to the feelings of being aroused . . . and finding pleasure in those feelings. Yet, the aching can grow too big, the desire too powerful. My body yearns for release.

It happened once this summer. A morning cuddle with her awakened my passion. Wanting more and knowing she wasn't able, I moved away to start my day. Soon, however, the summer heat mounted until all that was possible was to lie still, in a shady place. She and I found ourselves nude, in the downstairs of our cabin. She took to the hammock that hung across the room. I lay on the futon that serves as sofa on the floor. I tried to focus on a book, but in vain. My thoughts kept centering on making love with her. Soon, my eyes moved toward her, outstretched in the hammock. I began to fantasize about merging with the heat of the day, our own bodies' heat that would come from making love.

This fantasy, these thoughts, my desire grew stronger and stronger. I so much wanted her to turn toward me, to read my mind, to want the same. But it was not to be. She seemed absorbed in the pleasure of her book.

And so, I turned to myself. I stood up and took from an adjacent chair a large piece of cloth. I draped it over my bare shoulder, its coolness a contrast to my own warmth, and walked quietly out the back door.

I stepped out from the shade of the cabin into the bright sun and intense heat. The land seemed empty. The heat had driven the many visiting wimmin and residents of this wimmin's land to find respite indoors. Glad not to be interrupted, I moved silently across the yard and up onto the rise behind the main house. Here, where the blackberry bush grew round and full like a beautiful large womon, and the horsetail reached my thighs; here, where the forested hillside above me brought shade and coolness to the ground below; here, I would lie down with myself.

My bed was the long, green wild grass whose tufts would give my head a pillow. I took the cloth from my shoulder and spread her open on the ground. She was a great, wide, oversized piece of material whose rich orange-red background was woven through with an elaborate pattern in deep gold, evoking the quality of a beautiful tapestry. She was soft and smooth to the touch, quite like satin though not so stiff. Having had her in my life for years, yet never quite knowing how best to use her, I was now amused and delighted that she would hold me in these moments of lovemaking.

This spot I had chosen was far enough away from the houses and garden that I could hear no voices. I relaxed in the knowing that these moments were mine, a gift to myself. I would lie here undisturbed and experience the deliciousness of my own body's loving of herself.

I lay down, stretching out my long frame onto this beautiful familiar red cloth. Again, the coolness of the fabric contrasted with the heat of my body. Above me were the dark green branches of the mama blackberry and the clear, blue summer sky. My hands, with oh, such lovely care and attention, moved across my body, touching and stroking all the places that bring me pleasure.

And when my body had been satiated, I pulled the sides of my cloth-friend over me because I wanted to feel held and protected. I lay there, deeply relaxed, fully nourished, happy to be alive. I could smell the dark, rich earth under me and watched as my breath made the wild weed grass dance beside me.

Soon, I would walk back across the sun-draped yard, into the house where she would be . . . and she would look up smiling, light shining from her lovely sea-green eyes. Perhaps she would reach out with those strong, gentle hands that I so love. Perhaps I would walk over to kiss her warm forehead with my now cool lips.

And I would recognize that by gifting myself with myself, I could then receive the gifts she offered freely. And sometimes, it didn't have to be difficult at all. I stood up, wrapped my orange-red cloth around me, and started home.

The Haunting

Christina Springer

Enter a pause in ripening. The place where stretch marks are morning glories crawling, firm roots entrenched, deep in mocha-caramel pudding bellies. This momentary pause between the times of frivolity in youth and the silent halt of age. The time of sensuality devoted to baby dolls and building blocks.

This pause was equal in magnitude of rocking tent revivals to chastity. The bells ring out the gospel of virginity in motherhood. Complacency gusts sand dunes over memory of touch, careless toying in intimacy. The perceived veil, madonna blue, bursts hymnals where brusque moans previously made love songs in leather wrist restraints. Watch the young girl, nipples bare to the sunlight on a whimsical dare, decompose without heed to warning. This is the pause on which I sat.

I welcomed memory into this pause. It had been five years ago that we had parted, the precision of the date uncanny. We had left love on the eclipse of perfection. This eclipse made bright by fingers singing burnt coffee nipples into boil. Our dissolution raging with passion. She, the consumer of unyielding desire, caressed my body. Her fingers rumbling this mocha field into full bloom produced an uncanny aching into a present-tense pause. She had taught a lesson about wanting. She, the ruthless teacher, forced desire to peak without plateau. The evening of dissolution, she whispered into my ear, "The leaving of love on the doorstep of its ultimate perfection has a tendency to render memories of unsurpassable paragons in eternity." She had a way of making words shudder across the mind as curse or premonition.

On this pause in ripening, I denied the danger of beckoning memory. The conjuring of reckless maidens in youth, while dangerous, droops placidly in the face of excitement on this pause. This had been our essence, reckless concern to meet face to face with youth in ravishing each other through hours of souls and bodies as arcs. Casting the consummate intensity of being locked in union, we knew we would carry these memories forever . . .

* * * * * *

The darkness of storm on a full moon raged outside of Katy's uncurtained windows. The shadows of two red candles teased and flirted the illusion of protection from the storm against terra cotta walls. Katy believed in the womb. Her two room apartment simultaneously lay open to outside intrusion while the warmth of its darkness seemed as contained and inviting as herself.

She didn't believe in furniture. Oversized pillows, a table, two chairs and king size bed were the only concession to the obligatory comfort of guests. Her most prized acquisition, the snake cage, glowed an eerie blue against the yellow light of the candles. This evening Pavlova was as disturbed as the elements. Her tongue darted in and out as she cajoled her eight foot body into marking the corners of her glass home. Pavlova's black eyes peered at us, unclothed and wrapped around one another on the bed. She and her forked tongue were a disturbingly exciting complement to the bedroom.

My cheek nestled against Katy's breast, I tilted my head to take in the face that so moved me. This was our last night together. I wanted to memorize the way the imperceptible down on her cheek made me glide my hand along her cheekbone. This tracing compelled my hand to graze the edge of her ear only to find itself travelling across her jawline en route to her neck. I needed to guarantee memory of the way the curve of her lips called forth a finger to trace their outline. The way those succulent strawberries on her breasts begged to be relished, with tongue pressing and pulling a sigh of desire. Katy stared at the ceiling, the silence of this moment comforting. A cigarette dangled from rose lips. Her hand, fingers long and tapered, grasped the cigarette between thumb and index finger, dispatching it towards the ashtray, as my tongue flashed across her nipple.

From the first time I had met her, standing behind the counter of the five-and-dime store, I knew she was one of the White women with strawberry and cream bodies. I had a compulsion to experience these women. Somehow, I had always found myself drawn to the boudoir of lanky long White women with strawberry and cream bodies. I had stared through her shirt, absent-mindedly paying for a pack of gum. I was contentedly married to a mocha-caramel amazon. The passionately intimate match would last a lifetime, regardless of antique Victorian novels and the burning image of rosy nipples. Yet, for a year I had consistently found myself stealing away to enjoy strawberries and cream. "And so here we are," I mused aloud more to Pavlova than Katy, "with our tongues darting out in search of a tasty morsel." Katy's laugh entwined itself around a gasp deep in her throat, as I nipped at her strawberry nipples.

Katy rolled over on top of me. Her hands pinned my wrists to the bed. Her shoulders, an exquisite landscape of hills and valleys, loomed above me. My tongue traced this horizon, glistening and salty in the heat of this summer storm. "I want to make you a memory for the air," she asserted into the twilight of the room. "I want you to lay still, so you will remember."

Katy's hands heavy on my wrists sent a thrill of longing reverberating a spiral unfolding from my clit on through the leaping of my heart and quickening of my breath. Her thigh pressed against my vulva, and again. Her hips danced a jazz riff against my clit, my back arching to force my hips to lock into this pulsing rhythm. Our bodies pressed a release against each other. Our breath, quick and furious, matched the wind outside. We rocked against each other, my legs tight around each of hers between mine, toes pointed with the tension of passion ripping through me. Her nipple, now rosy, ridged and hard, poised daring my mouth to take it in. My tongue flickered against it, luxuriating in her fullness. I could feel her wetness paint a glistening veneer on my thigh.

Her body retreated from my touch. "I want you to lay still," she whispered in my ear, her tongue brushed fleeting against my ear lobe, teasing me to attention. Then the slight sensation of teeth bending in the flesh punctuated her whisper. "I want you to remember. I want you to remember wanting." Her tongue outlined the curve of my neck, my heart pounding, aching desire ripped through my body. I wanted her. I needed her to end this need for release. My mouth opened slightly to assure I would always remember this wanting. Her mouth settled on mine, lips open and ready; she plunged her tongue inside, trapping a moan that would have been words.

I wanted her, my hips taking in this kiss surged against her dewy lips opening, our bodies covered in a shining glow of summer passion. Her lips opened, the ephemeral notion of sensing the smooth, round, pulsing of her clit against me passed across my mind, delirious with want. The seizure of passion shooting pangs of desire clamoring to release overwhelmed me. I could tell she, too, was searching to unravel this quest for completion.

The pressure on my wrists eased. She unpinned me to search for something on the floor. Katy smoked in bed, waving a red flag at intimacy, as if time were disposable like diapers. Turning back to face me with a cigarette in her mouth, she extended one to me. I did not think I could inhale smoke with a chest heaving rapidly up and down, my body tense with urgency. Yet I took the offering, my smile and vapid eyes eliciting a frivolous amused chuckle. "Patience builds character," she teased, "I don't think you're ready to show me how much you can want. You need to wait." She lighted the cigarette in my mouth. Her fingers toyed with the curve under my breast. A cigarette in her fingers, she patterned circles on my breast, spiraling in to the burnt-coffee nipple, puckered and firm. She pinched my nipple, the orange tip of the cigarette dangerously close to my skin producing a sharp gasp. She smiled, "A little hot?" Her amusement was relished as possessively as rare antiques. She was intrinsically the most quintessential consumer of desire. Every sound penetrating the atmosphere in love fed her need to replenish the souls who forget to want.

Even her inadvertent movements were executed with unconscious calculation towards effect. Her hand stroked the edge of the tangled kinky garden above my punani. Tickling and teasing, while calmly she drew in smoke and promptly discharged it. Unable to keep my wits about me, I disposed of the cigarette in the ashtray on my side of the bed. Katy reached over, brushing against my nipple to flick an ash carelessly in the direction of my ashtray, then paused. She looked into me, as only sylphs can, to open the gateway to your soul by passing through the door in your eyes, "The only thing I want from you is to let me love you. Completely."

The storm must have calmed. The moon was shining full and serene in her window. Pavlova lay motionless in her cage. "Are we boring you Pavlova?" she said elusively, unresponsive to me panting next to her. She turned back to me, "See, Pavlova wouldn't mind if you abandon yourself." The glow of moonstone, her arms, illuminated by windows without curtains, cradled my neck. She traced my face, as I had wanted to do to her earlier. Her voice reverberated softly against my eardrums, a quaint encircling of sound, "I want you to want." Her cheeks, an imperceptible down, brushed against mine as her lips searched the depths of my own, parted, too.

"I want you to remember wanting," she said, as her hand traced the side of my body, ready for her every whim. She laid my head gently back against the pillow, peering down at me, "I love the way your locks fan out across the pillow." She kissed my forehead, whispering, "Will you?" She pressed her hand between my thighs, "Will you do that for me? Will you? Will you remember wanting?" I nodded my head, eyes glazed. "I'm glad." Her finger, featherlike, courted my throbbing clit. Hips bobbing back and forth, her touch catapulted my body up from the pillow. She caught my head in her arm. Cradled against her, my hand, caught in her hair, pulled her in for a kiss. As she plunged her tongue inside of my mouth, her hand entered the cavern of my body, drenched with the need to be filled. Her thumb vibrated against my throbbing clit, sending me reeling into a frenzy. Deep inside me, filling, fulfilling, tickling and teasing a promise of yielding to pleasure. She took me. Coaxed my body until the waves started to flow a rainbow through my belly. A scream of release heaved from my throat, penetrating the silence of the night. She cradled my convulsing body, still shaking from satisfaction, gently kissed my eyes, my cheeks, until waves ceased to rattle my body.

She had plunged inside the essence of my absolute need. She had captured her own desire for my need from me. Tentatively, my hand searched the curve of her breast. Her hands, glistened with passion, firmly grasped my own. "Just remember," she said, laying me down on the pillow. I looked into the green eyes and smiled.

A peculiar exercise in disparity was this last night together. My wife had been transferred to a new state. I would follow. This end was a natural completion to straying outside the confines of matrimony. It had been a sojourn in the remnants of a cycle. I would soon opt to house new life in this body, settling for the ultimate commitment. We had not had an easy time maneuvering these moments. It had felt as if the concept of honesty and fidelity were riddled with paradox verging on hypocrisy. Theoretically, I was free to pursue. In practicality, I was expected and demanded to be home. Yet there was a passing Katy would facilitate. There was a need for a last journey. A rendering of unsurpassable paragons to possess.

The phone screamed its intrusion. Katy rolled over to answer it. I lay curious, watching, smoking a cigarette. Katy looked over towards me. "Haven't seen her," she said into the phone. "Yeah, I'm kind of busy tonight. If I see her I'll tell her." She hung up the phone, turning to me, "That was Sali. Your wife called from Pennsylvania expecting you home." I sat up. Katy's hands on my shoulders eased me back onto the bed. "No big deal, you can call her from here."

"My doña, mia compañera, always searching to keep me out of trouble." I smiled at Katy's laughter. Sali had somehow always gained prominence in my intimate life. Sali propelled me towards suitable matches, clucking and cawing over this woman and that. Then, once happily settled with her vision of the appropriate match, proceeded to protect my commitment for me. With Sali's approval, I had married Jennifer. Sali became a ferocious protector of us both. Typically she succeeded in preventing me from straying. Katy had eluded her. Sali and I had gone everywhere together for years. Her commitment to friendship extended itself to include Jennifer. The three of us built a household together. Sali and I lived together, worked together, played together, until I had met Katy. Sali had wanted Katy to make a partner for doubles. It hadn't worked that way. Somehow I found myself with both Jennifer and Katy.

Sali was bold and daring to my shyness. She had put Katy and me together in spite of ourselves. The first time we had seen Katy together prompted Sali to maneuver frequent trips to the five-and-dime, often three times in a day. Sali would flirt, I would become confused and coy, staring through her shirt to my imagining of strawberries and cream. The day Sali noticed a silver labarys nicking the collarbones of Katy's neck, she had invited her out for drinks. Sali was an extraordinary extravert. She would ask anything from anybody interesting to her. I could barely put forth a hello. Sali and I were a dynamic duo.

Every day, in lieu of proceeding directly home from work, we stopped for drinks at the bar with Katy. Sali arranged evenings at the bar unaware of what she had provided. Jennifer hated to dance. She preferred to stay home. Committed to this marriage at an early age, I was seemingly always in the company of a chaperon while accumulating youthful memories.

Soon Sali's presence over the flirting match of licking salt from margaritas became an archaic game in preventing adultery. It felt trite within the confines of a modern day lesbian feminist relationship. Yet Jennifer was quite confident in Sali's watchful eye. Sali and I would meet Katy at the bar. That night Katy had cornered me without Sali between us.

There I was, back to the wall, feeling the brush of black jeans against my sheer gypsy skirt. There she was, pretending at speaking above the speakers and the confusion of flashing lights, whispering, "I want you." I smiled, flushed with her honesty. I wanted her, too, but I would not have admitted it. She brought her knee up between my legs, her body holding me to the wall. "Well?" she whispered into my burning ears.

"Well, what Katy?" It was all I could respond to her breasts grazing my gauze shirt. Her knee pressing against my vulva. Her arms making a curtain around me. She leaned into me, her cheek a whisper against mine. She dared to bend in, kissing my neck. My breath grew short, as the glow between my legs responded. I could not.

"I want you." She said it again, quite simple, factual, as if she were discussing the weather. "What do you want?" Her leg began to rub against me in time to the music. I couldn't keep my hips from answering for me. I just nodded my head, blushing. There in the bar, against the wall, wondering whether I would be discovered, she made excitement peak to passion. In a bar, that curious ripple of explosion made my body sink against hers in release for the first time.

Katy's tongue on my nipple brought me from this memory. My fingers travelled through her short hair. "I was thinking about that night at The Niche." She smiled and looked up.

"You were such a prude." she laughed, sitting up.

"I was not!" I sat to face her. Her arms clasped around my shoulders pulled me backwards on top of her body. I knew it had been true.

"You were. You wanted me, but wouldn't admit it," she teased.

I peered into her green eyes. My tongue traced the curve of her lips. I gently pried them open, thrusting my tongue deep inside of her. Timidly, my tongue caressed the ridge of her collarbone, the map guiding me to trace infinity across her nipple, her hips wriggling their enjoyment. I followed the map to the gentle fuzz of her pubis, the plain of her belly making the journey delicate. Her belly shivered a saltiness, her hand urging me towards my destination. My tongue flicked along the line of fluffy blonde hair, teasing a jump from her hips. I toyed with the rosebud of her clit, pink and shiny, peering out from yielding lips, then lost myself en route elsewhere, the insides of her thighs, a creamy elixir, soft and smooth. "See, I'm not a prude." I retorted.

"Not anymore," she said as my tongue circled her clit, her hips an arc of pleasure. She bucked against my mouth, licking a wild dance to her passion. She sighed, eyes closed, neck arched back. Her legs tensed, one foot pointed with ecstasy curled over my back as I relished her succulent juices. Silently I slid a finger inside of her, thrusting deep against the furious sucking determined to overtake her body with abandonment to want. Her hands, tangled in my locks, pressed my face to her. I was eager to drink her in, greedily pressing my tongue against her clit until she pushed me away, moaning incoherently.

We rolled through each other over and over again that night. Each giving in to the other's need. She making me confess to want. My wanting her to yield to my touch.

"I want you." She said it repeatedly over the course our year together. Being wanted, more powerful than the passion itself, was crucial to gaining spiritual kinship to willow trees. She had imposed on each delicate sensibility. She had ripped modesty and convention from each fingernail clinging to decency. After this time with her, where the clothing of a prudish miser of love boasts a flagrant trail towards the bed, I was ready. I had experienced three hundred and sixty-five revolutions of being wanted.

We had both come together as complimentary colors placed honestly in a painting for the enhancement of the overall picture. She craving to devour martyrdom, I needing to be wanted, stood looking over the waterfall of ended paths. We had most certainly built a memory for the air that night.

The next morning she stood at her closet door, slipping black jeans over white socks, as she had each time. I arched towards the red lace bra, then sat up dancing the lingerie tango. She slipped her feet into black penny loafers, swung her coat through the air to stave off the chill outside. She did not say good bye, or dictate instructions about keys; only, "To think about someone is to knock on the door of their soul."

* * * * *

Having dangled over the cliff that begins the waterfall, I settled into domesticity. Sali had stayed behind with my secret. I had earned my degree of love, I required no additional research. Jennifer had seemingly remained ignorant to this dedicated accumulation of knowledge over the course of the year. Even had I laid open the quest for want, she would not really have exercised undue concern for passing fancy. The larger political ramifications of finding oneself vexed about affairs was irrelevant to her concept of progressive lesbian relationships. It was the concept of moving outside personal boundaries, to grow in privacy, that was the thrill . . .

* * * * *

Katy only came over the telephone wire after that day when she returned to her solitude and I to my marriage. I believe her words to have been the precursor of binding us together throughout destiny. The calls never came from her. I would periodically feel urged to deposit large sums of money in the accounts of the telephone company. We would talk. She would tease. I would feel a wetness begin to flow and maneuver the conversation towards diapers and baby talk.

Yet I proceeded, posting signs bidding welcome. I continued to include her in my thoughts. One day her image floated across my mind, hands plunged into the tedium of dishes. I knew she was knocking on the door of my soul. To issue invitation to enter, long after consent has been revoked, is to place that soul in the precarious fluctuation of conflicting emotions. There is the time when invitation unmarked on a calendar floods the attention of entirety in being. Her presence became unshakable. It was haunting and elusive. I took to this haunting with contrary impulsiveness characteristic of women on the precipice.

We had been parted for over five years. I was enraptured with the way her hand still reached into my dreams. The way she haunted this need to feel with intent. A hand twisting deep inside with the swirling push against want yielding to release of rapture caged. She would come to me as I slept, pressing the memory we had built for air to the forefront of my dream world. Each morning I emerged towards the yellowing light of surface, drenched in the tangible response of willing concubine resuscitated.

She tapped politely at my door for five years. I opened it, a slit placing barrier to need, hesitating at making a commitment to licentiousness or relief confined. A crumb of welcome graciously bestowed incited her to seize and purge this cloistered me subsiding in neglect. She seeped through, her blast of decision forcing my own. This trait she revered, commanding control of reservation to give concretely to abandon. She laid me open, disregarding the game of clenched purity craving pursuit in ramming the ebb of slipping in love through colors of release. She consumed desire, a habit once endearing, now annexed memory to a waking self wet with pleasure.

She was addict and drug. She had forced herself into dreams. Dreams that could be played off as a pardonable fantasy conceived during indulgence to subconscious ramblings. This was not enough. She had never been content to echo passing nightly fancies. She began to meander about my mind sitting on too small chairs praising two-year-old drawings. A melancholy humming to the girl now fully decomposed would flirt dare for me to chase myself.

Still, I wanted it. I had to have this haunting. I hesitated to reach to her. Conflicted by perfection and illusion, I faltered. I would be sitting at the dinner table, distracted and overwhelmed, the feeling would rush over me, a flush of heat dripping. My clit began to pulse, as her hand through space would cajole and caress. The pushing, pressing against my thighs would come again, the entering of her hand, the thrust of focus to her cleansing me of thought. Then a hushed startled moan of release. At first she would leave me to amused questioning faces. I knew she smiled all those miles away, and, satisfied, I would do the same.

I had every Madison Avenue image in my life, the few alterations to my own liking. Jennifer was mocha-caramel like me. We had moved past this honeymoon to parenthood. Our child, dark and sweet, had become central to our lives. Jennifer was the sketch of womanhood I had pulled into reality, the glistening sweet and tart taste of suburban living distinctly congruous to my vision. Not since Katy had I found the need to pursue strawberry and cream women. I had sunk myself into the entirety of our perfection.

Yet I was compelled to continue a non-existent affair across miles. I entered a self-manufactured Lent, fasted righteously on virtuousness. Feeling no need for repentance, she continued to beg a yield.

I gave, I couldn't help it. I gorged myself on lost time. She gleefully humored this need. Penetrated me with flutter of caresses, repeatedly refusing to cease this inundation of excitement until I took to my bed, satisfied, exhausted. The giggle of release bubbling insanity to love consummated across hundreds of miles.

Every snippet of resistance winnowed away, I lay in my bed, eyes glazed as she poured thrill into me. Jennifer became concerned. I had no desire to lift myself out of bed. I had no more wondering of the ethics and affect on family. I lay passively, as she filled me with herself, marvelling at the constant glory of her ardent touch.

Her tongue would press through space encircling my clit. My legs would sprawl apart, hips twisting. As the wet softness danced and toyed a constant pressure of pleasure. Hands brushing across my nipples, I moaned and tossed with abandon. Then the pressure inside, filling me, as the slip of tongue revealed a scream of satisfaction. I would lie in bed exhausted and smiling. Finally, saturating my consciousness, she departed. I felt her float away. I had given her all my desire. She drifted away complete.

We ask to be loved. We ask to want and be wanted. This, a seemingly innocent request, can give way to an understanding of what it is to embrace self. There is a time, having entered a passage of ripening, we feel obsolete in the knowing of sensuality. We perceive the girl decomposed, not resurrected; ignorantly shed tears for the death we need to embrace as gift she leaves behind. This haunting had been teacher. I had gratefully accepted the wisdom of opening to passion, of opening self to want and learn the pleasure of wanting. I could become the teacher.

To want, and to be wanted, without care or concern for image and pretense was a lesson I could bring to my home. We pause under the mundane and become buried. To think about someone is to knock on the door of their soul. I thought of Jennifer.

Relax, Enjoy

Emma Joy Crone

As I walked up to the small cottage I was aware of a feeling of great peace, tempered with some trepidation. A sensation of relaxing thoroughly, sights were of a profusion of flowers, every ledge held a small pot or vase, in which rested all the colors of summer. The smells that invaded my senses too, assisted in my final capitulation, lavender from a hugh bush near the door, roses tumbling over their frame. I stood inhaling, feeling the warm sun on my body, catching glimpses of the ocean through the fir and arbutus that surrounded the garden.

Was it the woman standing before me, or all of the above? As I stood at the entrance to her cottage I was aware of her standing in the doorway, smiling, her sometimes green, sometimes yellow eyes laughing into mine, demanding that I look at her, as I glanced about chattering and praising the beauty of her garden. Until today I'd kept my distance. I was feeling a mite scared to get into any sort of close scene with a woman again. After four years of celibacy, chosen out of fear of intimacy, and at 62 years old, I was feeling it was time to let go of all that hassle of being 'in love.' And here was this 35 year old, blatantly flirting and making me feel I could allow myself to open up again. We'd met at an acquaintance's house a few weeks earlier. I liked her direct way of relating, her casual air, her roguish manner, but most of all I enjoyed her warmly open, caring way with those around her.

Today I'd decided to drop by on my way to our store on the Island, and take the risk of meeting her again, to see if my initial reaction would re-occur.

"Come in," she urged. "I'm just taking a break from a cabinet I was making. We can enjoy some iced tea together."

"Thanks, I will, but I'm not staying long. I'm on my way to the Coop." I tried not to let my feelings of delight creep into my voice. I was trying hard not to look at her neat, compact body, tight T-shirt revealing her pointy, small breasts. She was a carpenter by trade, and her muscles, which she would flex in a teasing way, made me want to run my hands over their suppleness. Soft brown hair curled round her face and I longed to reach up and caress the tendril at her ear.

I knew I wanted to love and be loved by this woman! We looked into each others eyes, the tea forgotten.

"I want you," she said, the teasing all gone out of her eyes. Her arms encircled me, I felt her strong, warm hands burning through my thin silk blouse.

Still, my fears reached out and clutched at me—was I ready for this—as I felt my body reacting to her caresses, was my libido betraying me? Her hardened nipples pressed into my breasts, a shudder of delight ran through me. So my sexuality was still capable of being aroused. Those four years of denial were being slowly and methodically challenged by the feelings that were surging through my body.

I felt her breath tickling my ear, her lips moving slowly down my throat to the hollow of my collar bone. I gasped.

"Hadn't we better go right inside?" she said, as we still lingered in the doorway. A smile tilted the corner of her mouth.

Taking my hand, she led me to a couch situated in a nook, the skylight above and windows surrounding letting in the sunlight and more views of her lovely garden. We sank into the softness of this, her bed, arms entwined around each other. Her fingertips gently caressed my hardening nipples. My mind was trying to react, but desire was winning. How could I resist when wave after wave of passion surged through my body? Frantically, I thought, is this love or lust?

"Relax. Enjoy," she whispered.

"Have you been tested for AIDS?" I stuttered, making a last ditch stand. I remembered in a sudden flash how I'd fended men off by saying I didn't want to get pregnant. Was I using this ploy once again? She laughed and briefly described her sexual encounters, meanwhile her hands danced over my body bringing me to heights of desire that left me weak. The barriers finally fell as her mouth closed over mine, her hand sliding over my stomach and down, down to my enlarging clitoris.

My juices flowing, I allowed myself to succumb, little dreaming that this passionate encounter would be the beginning of a hot and heavy affair that was destined to last. My libido, after all my fears of entrapment, was to be a source of joy and passion once again.

A Matter of Fact

Rocky Gámez

"Well, Gloria, how did it go last night?" Pinny asked as we were riding to Padre Island.

Gloria chuckled in the driver's seat and made noises with her wet lips as though she were savoring something very delicious. "I gave her eighteen orgasms," she said, smacking her lips, and then began bouncing up and down on the seat, singing: "Sha-la-la-la-la-la-la......"

"Eighteen orgasms!" I gasped from the back seat.

"You better believe it! And I left her crying for more."

"Aaaaharharrharr!" Pinny broke out with her ear-piercing laughter. "And if you believe that, little pebble, I've got a date for you with Pedro Infante."

I shook my head in disbelief and joined Pinny in mocking laughter. "Why do I have trouble believing that?" I asked Gloria, wiping the moisture from my eyes.

"Because you've never been fucked by me," Gloria said in her usual cockiness.

Pinny roared again: "Aaaarrrharharharhar!" and I could see through the mirror Gloria's bushy eyebrows knitting with displeasure. If there was something Gloria couldn't take very well it was the ridicule we always orchestrated when we didn't believe her stories. "Cheesus Criss! Eighteen orgasms! Does she run on some kind of batteries? I've been fucking since I was six years old and I've never gotten anything but one at the most."

"That's because you fuck guys," Gloria said, breathing hard because she was getting angrier and angrier with us. "Guys don't know the first thing about pleasing a woman."

"And you do! Pinny continued. "Aaaarrrharharhar! *Qué desgraciada eres!*"

"Eighteen orgasms on the average, and that is a matter of fact!"

Pinny broke up again, slapping her thighs several times.

"How could you keep count, Gloria?" I wanted to know, and I was being perfectly honest. At the time I didn't know the first thing about being sexual, but what I had been told by those two insofar as losing one's mind while in the throes of passion, it just didn't seem possible to me. "Do you carry an automatic counter with you? Or do you cut notches on the bedpost, or what?"

Gloria didn't answer. I could feel her dander rising. And knowing what she was capable of doing when the mercury of her temper rose, I decided to drop the subject with a quick, "Sorry I asked," apology. We were already too far away from home and I didn't want to walk back. But Pinny was never one who knew when to stop.

She kept on ribbing Gloria: "Eighteen orgasms! Cheesus Criss! Eighteen orgasms! I'd like to know what kind of diet she's on."

Gloria drove in dark huffy silence.

"Hey, Rocky, make this eighteen orgasms one of the chapters to your Gloria Stories. Make every fucker and fuckee blush with ineptitude when they read it. Aaaarrrharharhar!"

Oh, I wanted to howl with laughter, too, but I knew better. If the two of us had ganged up on Gloria in mockery she would've thrown us out of her car, and it would not have been the first time either. One time she had dumped us near Corpus Christi and we had hitchhiked our way back to the Valley with fallen arches and blisters on our heels. So I kept my mouth shut. Besides not wanting to walk, I had a more important need to get to the beach. My biology project had to be completed that weekend and I still needed some more sea shell specimens to finish it.

"*Ya, Pinny, cállate el hosico!*" I suggested.

But she wouldn't drop it. She was still howling and carrying on when we got to the beach where Gloria's two new friends were waiting for us.

I had never seen those two women before. Gloria said she had met them on her broom-selling route somewhere in Raymondville. They were married to each other since they were both teenagers.

One of them was a tall and skinny affair with long dark hair that came down to her waist. Gloria called her Vitola because she had a very strong resemblance to the Mexican comedienne of the same name. The other one was a short mannish woman that introduced herself as Ernest but I never knew whether that was short for Ernestina or Ernest Borgnine whom she resembled enough to be his twin brother. Needless to say, they both gave me the creeps instantly, although I had no specific reason since I am never one to judge anyone on the first look. It was just an uncomfortable feeling, especially with Ernest who didn't really look at a person, but leered instead. But as I said, my trip to the beach was simply to finish my biology project, not to socialize with Gloria's new friends. Pinny noticed my squirming right away, and as soon as we got our stuff from the trunk of the car, she hooked an arm around mine and said: "Come, little pebble, let's go hunt for your precious shells before it gets dark." She threw a quick glance over her shoulder and snickered at Gloria. "Eighteen orgasms! Aaarrrharharhar! *Qué desgraciada.*"

When we returned with my pockets and a paper bag filled with a stash of sea shells, the sun had already gone down and most of the crowd at the beach had left. Gloria and her two peculiar friends were sitting around the fire they had built. The sweltering heat had subsided and a gentle cool breeze had begun to blow inland. I went to the trunk of Gloria's car to put away my newly acquired treasures of the sea and slipped into my jeans and parka. I didn't want to be with those people because I could feel Ernest's watery eyes all over me. As I was skirting around the car to walk along the beach by myself, I overheard Gloria saying to Ernest, "Forget her, man. She don't fuck anyone."

I had a feeling Gloria's pronouncement was in reference to me and I was glad that she was putting the record straight. I sat alone on the beach, watching the enormous moon creeping over the Gulf, wondering how I would react if that horrific bulldyke decided to pursue my company. She surely gave me the impression that she always got what she wanted one way or another. She seemed so sure of herself, so rough and tough macho, that I was sure she ate nails and shat crowbars. And what could I say to her should she not take Gloria seriously? There was something so unappealing about that mannish woman that the thought of having her near me was embarrassing.

Many people in the barrio thought the same thing about Gloria and had often asked me why she and I were ever friends. But Gloria, mannish as she was, too, was never that repulsive to me, otherwise I would've never been as drawn to her as I was. Gloria was different, funny, and there was an appealing innocence about her despite her pathological affliction for sex. She had never, since I had known her, made any advances toward me nor tried to lay her persuasions on me either. We were just friends and I had always believed her when she said, "I never fuck my friends."

I was trying to think about what it was that made me feel such a strong discomfort for that person Ernest, trying to make a comparison between her and Gloria, when I heard Pinny coming up behind me. "Aaaarrrrharharhar!"

"Man, you should hear the stories Gloria and Ernest are telling each other," she said, sitting next to me. "Eighteen orgasms are fairy tales to Ernest."

When I didn't answer her, she said, "They're going to fuck Vitola soon as it gets dark and everyone else has left the beach."

"Oh, gross!"

Pinny nodded and lighted a cigarette. I could sense her discomfort by the way she was blowing smoke. "I don't like that woman, Ernest. She gives me the creeps. Both of them do. Vitola is just like her pet dog, does anything she asks her to."

Long after Pinny had returned to the fire with the others I made a sand woman out of the mound of sand we had both dug. She was life-size with well-rounded hips and big breasts, and an elevated mound to emphasize her womanliness. I was bending over her to give her two sand dollar eyes when suddenly I felt a presence behind me.

"Whatcha doin', kid?"

I didn't answer nor look up. I wanted her to go away. She had compounded her unpleasantness by being drunk.

"Gloria says you've never had sex with anyone."

"Gloria's right," I said in a curt tone that was intended to be unfriendly.

"Would you like me to teach you how?" she insisted, squatting next to the sand woman I had just formed, a bottle of beer in hand and a cigarette hanging from her mouth.

I shook my head negatively, not wanting to even look her in the eye. She was so frightening, I wanted to flee into the ocean and let the piranhas get to me before I allowed her to touch me.

At that moment the other three joined us. I was never so glad to see Gloria as I was then. Since I had known her I had always felt safe in her company, knowing that she would never let anything happen to me that I didn't want to happen. It was not the first time I had been in that predicament.

"Well," Gloria said to the woman, "shall we flip a coin to see who starts first with Vitola?"

Pinny exploded with her loud laughing in the background, frightening a pair of gulls that were gliding over our heads.

A Matter of Fact 39

"Aaaarrrrharharhar! Flip a coin, she says! Like they were going to have a contest."

"Shut your big snout, Agripina! I've had it with your horse laugh."

"You two are so full of shit! You're acting like the worst kind of men."

"I don't want to do it in front of that girl," Vitola said, sullenly.

Ernest gave her a dirty look and the skinny woman squirmed as if she had put her foot in her mouth.

"I won't do it! I won't do it!"

"Why not?" Ernest growled, flinging the empty beer bottle aside. "You've done worse."

"I don't care what I've done before. I have my limits and this girl's nerdy presence is where I draw the line." She took a couple of steps back, then sprinted towards the two cars which were quite a distance away.

Gloria grabbed Ernest by her sleeve. "Let her go, man! If she don't want to do it, it's okay by me."

"Well, it's not okay with me! She said she would and she will, goddamn it. I'm the boss in this family, *pos que no ni que la chingda.*" She tore herself from Gloria's grip and went after her friend. When she was out of sight, I turned to Gloria, angry as a hornet.

"What the hell do you think you're doing? What makes you think I want to see you doing your *chingaderas?*"

"She wants you to see how great she is at fucking so you'll write it in her story. That's why," Pinny said in an accusatory voice.

"That's not true," Gloria said, bending her knee next to my sand woman.

"Get away from my woman, *pinche culera!*"

Ernest returned without Vitola. She was livid with rage because the other woman had out-run her toward the shower stalls where there was a crowd of people waiting to go into the showers. She came and stood in front of us with her legs apart, huffing and puffing, trying to look more macho than earlier. "I still think I'm a better fucker than you'll ever be," she said to Gloria, and then she sauntered up to me. "You want to do it with me so I can show Gloria?"

"Get away from her!" Pinny shrieked. "Gloria, make her stop!"

Gloria got between us, trying to push Ernest away from me. "No, Ernest," she said, "not this one. Leave her out of it."

But Ernest wouldn't back off. "Just let me kiss you once and I bet you'll open up to me right here in front of God and everybody else."

"She said no!" Pinny yelled angrily. "Gloria, make her stop. It's your horny fucking fault! Stop it, you weird peculiar thing, you!"

At that moment Gloria grabbed her from behind and brought her down on the sand with a loud thud, right on top of my beautiful sand masterpiece, where they began wrestling each other. Gloria was not angry at first, she was giggling, trying to keep the stronger-looking woman from getting up. It wasn't until Ernest kicked her on the groin that she turned purple. They went at each other like a pair of pit bulls, tearing at each other's clothes, beating each other with their fists. It was so disgusting I wanted to run to the shower stalls to get help. Both were very capable of inflicting a lot of damage to each other. Finally Gloria was able to pin Ernest down on the sand by straddling her and both Pinny and I sighed in relief. I don't know what would've happened had the reverse been true. But I was glad to see Gloria in the dominant position.

I had never seen Gloria as angry as she was that evening. She kept pouncing on that woman like she had gone crazy and no matter how much Pinny was pleading with her to stop, she was beyond reasoning.

She ripped Ernest's shirt off in angry, violent jerks, tossing the pieces of cloth aside while Pinny jumped up and down on the sand, crying, "Gloria, stop it! For God's sake, stop it! Have you gone crazy or what?"

I didn't know what to do. I ran to the top of a sand hill hoping to see someone who might come down to the beach to help us get Gloria off of Ernest, but there was no one in sight but Vitola, sitting like a human stump in the distance, smoking a cigarette.

When I returned to the battling site, Gloria was still straddling the older woman. She had her arms pinned to the sand, but Ernest wasn't struggling anymore. She seemed to just be laying there powerless in hopeless resignation.

Pinny, all pale and alarmed, ran behind me and began to squeeze my shoulders. "Rocky! Rocky! Gloria is going to fuck Ernest. Look at her moving on top of her!"

"Oh, gross!" I said. "Gloria, stop it!"

But Gloria had no ears for us anymore nor any concern about who might be coming up the beach from the darkness and stumble upon them in that undignified position. She moved on Ernest in undulating motions that left nothing to doubt. Then she unzipped Ernest's pants and introduced her entire hand into her crotch where she drew up a wad of something that resembled a pair of rolled up socks. Pinny said it was her fake balls, and it suddenly dawned on me that was what had turned me off right away about her, that bulge in front of her. But obviously it hadn't affected Gloria in the least.

She pulled down Ernest's khaki men's pants, her jockey shorts, and began to rub her hand on the woman's genitals. The woman's body began to heave slowly at first, then she began to tremble all over. It was time for me to make my exit.

"Oh, little pebble, please don't go away. I don't want to stay here by myself," Pinny said. "Don't you want to see how women do it?"

I walked away, shocked out of my puerile sensibilities. I had never seen anything like that before in my life, and I couldn't understand how that could be called "making love." Love, to me, had always been a feeling, a state of the mind, not that sudden expression of uncontrolled passion. It would be many years later before I would be able to understand the incident that night. I kept walking up the beach by myself, wanting to keep on walking until the end of the world, but I couldn't. The end of the world was shrouded in fog and I was too timid to go any further than I had already walked. I stopped at the walls of introspection and sat there for a while, wondering how some people could do that sort of thing without good feelings for each other. If I ever did that, it would have to be an expression of love and nothing less than that. The distance between my mind and my genitals would always be considerable. I knew then that that was what had really been the reason why I had been so repelled by Ernest and her lover, Vitola. Walking back, I wondered how I was going to feel about Gloria, later on.

They were still going at it. I could see the two darkened figures in the sand with two other silhouetted figures sitting there with their legs drawn up to their chin, watching intently. I went and sat next to Pinny, in front of Vitola and the glowing ash of her cigarette.

Ernest's legs were practically draped over Gloria's shoulders, and Gloria's face was right in the middle of things. They could have cared less had the Texas National Guard descended upon the beach at that moment. Ernest was moaning and groaning in complete abandon with Gloria like a pig at a trough filling herself with victory.

I wanted to say something but didn't know what except, "Do you have another cigarette with you, Agripina?"

She offered me the whole pack without taking her eyes off of the fucking twins. "Will you believe it?" she said in a hushed voice. "Gloria's made that woman come eighteen times! Cheesus Criss! And I thought she was full of shit!"

"And you've been sitting here counting?"

"I just wanted to see if it was true."

I drew my legs up to my chin, too, wondering how I was ever going to begin to write this if I ever set my mind to write the "Gloria Stories."

september

zana

your fingers on my clit . . . my fingers on your clit . . . i almost don't know which is which, what is what, who is whom, and . . . i melt into you in pure joy . . .
   wet, wet, wet, and i feel your clit rise and pulse under my fingers . . . i never felt that with anyone before, was never so sensitive, so present. and i'm thrilled, delighted, in love with your sweet clit who responds to me so nice . . .
   we started out with all our clothes on, slow, shy, slow. you shy, me needing slowness. rubbing against each other's thighs, yours in blue denim cutoffs, mine in long purple gauze. rubbing our clothed bodies together and kissing, oh, kissing. wet, wet. kissing and holding each other so hard, on my bed, with a fan on, in the heat of an arizona september morning, wearing tank tops and pants and finally you dared take off your top and i tore mine off too and flung it away. then your soft breasts came happily to mine.
   kissing, kissing . . . and i heard you unzip your pants— exciting sound! (in my mind, the zipper was heavy brass.) you grabbed my hand and slid it in. no underwear. your clit so fat and ready, and down in your hair, so wet, sweet love, so wet.
   afternoons, mornings, sometimes nights. our smiles, glowing. i love your love-smile, how different from what the world sees. so red and full and juicy. and your shining eyes.
   I love your eyes, hazel like mine but more brown and gold, while mine are greeny. like olives. olive—our skins together, like sisters. i have longed for that . . . kinship. i love your hair, in black waves against my cheek; i love the little black circles of hair decorating your cunt, the wet swirls under your arms. and the soft dark hair above your lips, that my lips sometimes feel, i love. i even like those black hairs on your chin, and in learning to love them, i learn to love my own.

zana

    i love you . . . and i can't say it. the words beat at my lips for release, and i can't. so afraid you don't want that, can't take it. i want to hear you say those words and you don't. so i don't. you say "oh honey, oh sweetie" and i drink your words like nectar. you cry "oh zana" and my name sounds so beautiful from your lips. when i breathe your name into your hair, holding, caressing, it is the only word i know for how perfect and unique you are.

    breathtaking . . . when we touch each other's faces, amazed . . . that such feelings exist, such oneness exists, such magic. all at once, all for us. all because we want it, we both wanted it—miraculously—at the same time.

    dream-time, slow-time . . . drifting between passion and calm . . . so many places in between. i love when you hold me and talk, tell me about your last lover and her little girl, tell me your theories about the letter *shin*, tell me about selling secondhand books, tell me your dreams and fears. i love you when we lie and talk . . . i feel partnered with you, like we will share our lives always just like this, drifting together.

    odd to think "always." all the ways we are different, our lives are so different, you in the city, me in the country, the focus of our politics, the food we eat, our daily lives . . . and yet—

    our daily lives, our disabilities, we are middle-aged jews, writers, passionate in work and politics . . . and toward each other . . . and i have bonded with you somehow—our bodies and spirits have greeted each other like old, deep friends . . .

    i am so full i could not get any fuller. my love for you spills out of my eyes and the pores of my skin . . . days apart from you a soft haze surrounds me, i am filled to overflowing and i lavish joy upon my landsisters.

    i want to know you into every corner of your life, the hard parts, too. i want to explore with you our differences, our samenesses. a grand adventure, one i never planned. never thought i'd take a city lover, a lover with a tv, a dog. i was looking for my clone.

    i want to grow with you, change, challenge, laugh and cry. be new. will you?

    i love you and i am afraid to speak it. afraid to say those big and scary words. what we all want and are all afraid of.

    face next to face—how i like it best—and my thigh feels your soft hair as you slide along me. i shift just a little to feel your thigh harder against my clit. into the space created, my hand sneaks, seeking. finding that warm wet plump eager womonness of you . . . my fingers hold firm as you make your pleasure against them . . .

when you make me come and i start to cry and you say "you're not sad?" and i smile and whisper "no" . . . it's because there really are no words, and i'm taken to a place where everything i thought i knew is shaken loose . . .

Maggie, Sex, and the Baby Jesus, Too

Julie Blackwomon

If apologies are in order for what happened that night after the office Christmas party, then Maggie Stephens, I apologize.
But you see, it wasn't my fault.
All right, I admit it. I've got this totally warped sense of humor. It first manifested itself when I was a child in Sunday school. That's what blew Maggie Steven's orgasm. I swear it was through no willful intent of my own.

As children of the pastor at First Zion African Methodist Episcopal Church, my sister Rena and I had to set an example. When Rena wanted to get back at me for something, she'd often wait until the Sunday school teacher's back was turned and then proceed to imitate the way Mrs. Beasley twitched her nose when she was anxious. When Mrs. Beasley turned back around to face the class again, Rena would be sitting there like the somber, well-behaved twelve year old of the pastor. I, the pastor's youngest by three years, would be trying desperately to suppress a grin. And I'd be all right, too, until Mrs. Beasley either twitched her nose again or asked me what was funny. Or told me to stop laughing. I'd try my best to straighten up by imagining somebody had kicked over the manger of the poor baby Jesus and left the infant wailing on the floor at the feet of the jackass and the three Wise Men. I tell you it was tough. Even at that, sometimes I succeeded and sometimes I got my little but irreverent butt spanked. Sometimes even imagining poor little Jesus nailed on the cross could not stop me from laughing. Not if I thought of something funny.

And I swear there was no defiance involved. I know Jesus don't play that. And even if Jesus did play, the right Reverend James Scott did not. And Reverend Scott had a thick barber's strap that adequately discouraged me and my sister from ever mixing or confusing pleasure with pain. I needed to make Maggie Stephens understand this.

I met Maggie at the small advertising agency where I work as copy writer. Maggie Stevens was office manager. We got to know each other well at the small space between the counter and the copier. At least three times during my first week of employment Maggie managed to drag her hand across my fanny when she shimmied past me between the counter and the copier. Our mammary glands got fairly well acquainted, too.

I, however, thought the woman was straight, so I just bade my hormones be still and went on about my business.

But then she invited me out for a drink and we talked a bit. I discovered I liked her. I didn't see a long-term relationship in our future, but she was a genuinely nice woman. She was white, but she had all her racism neatly tucked in and although she didn't consider herself a feminist, she had decent politics. I liked the woman, and she obviously had the hots for me, which I found flattering. By heterosexual standards I was too tall, too big and too gawky. People who are unkind might even call me fat. I liked the way Maggie made me feel as if looking at me could make her pants wet, even without my wearing a girdle.

We would flirt with each other over the heads of the heterosexuals in the office.

After a few months of flirting we went to this conference together and stayed in the same room. In the same bed. Soon Maggie's warm hands found her way onto my thigh. We kissed a few times. If I'd had a penis I might have punched a hole in the sheets at that Holiday Inn in beautiful downtown Seattle. But I still wasn't ready. I was still too used to a commitment around my Sex. Maggie, to her credit, did not push me, nor call me tease. And after a long time we both went to sleep with our arms around each other.

Then there was the office Christmas party. After they opened the eighth bottle of champagne, Maggie's Mumms told her to ask me to dance. My Chevas Regal, encouraged by my hormones, told me to accept. I never win an argument with my Chevas Regal.

So Maggie plastered her pelvis to mine and made my clitoris vibrate like a rubber band.

We left the party early.

And because we were still unwilling to admit we both wanted to "do it," Maggie invited me to her apartment "for coffee," so I could sober up. Maggie left her car in the parking lot and neither of us questioned the logic that made it okay for me to drive forty blocks past my apartment to drive Maggie home, drink a cup of coffee, then drive forty blocks back home again.

We left the party with our arms around each other, unconcerned that we would be the juicy gossip at least until the next office party. It was not our fault, however. It was just another torrid example of two good women once again felled by the double H: High and Horny.

Based solely on the intensity of my orgasm afterwards, I decided I would never again miss an office party.

So the Christmas party is how I finally ended up on black silk sheets in Maggie's queen-sized water bed. (I may never make love on white sheets again.)

And now I was about to make love to Maggie, and everything was fine. Until I noticed the chocolate colored dildo lying on the nightstand. I could of course have ignored it, but it piqued my curiosity. Besides, I admit to my own kink. I found it somewhat of a turn-on.

"Why do you have a brown dildo?" I asked.

"Because I like the color," Maggie said indignantly.

I dropped the subject.

About ten minutes after we discussed the dildo, Maggie asked me if I were game to try something different and I said, "All right." I want it understood, Maggie Stevens, that I tried.

Maggie and I were lying on black silk sheets on the water bed in her efficiency apartment. There were two silk lavender ropes tied from the bedpost, which might have been from a robe. After our dialogue about the dildo I decided I wasn't going to ask about the silk ropes. She wore a pair of black lace panties over her blonde pubic hair. I looked down at her. I was wearing only a chocolate smile.

"You think you could sorta — hold me down?" Maggie asked.

Sure," I said, and I straddled her waist and held her down by her wrists. "Is this right?" I asked.

"I want to get up, now," she said. She also wore a leather collar and a pair of six inch black pumps. Yes, even in bed she wore the pumps. But this was her orgasm we were working on now. I'd already gotten mine. I leaned up on my elbow and stared down at her with a dreamy look in my eyes. I was very high. This may explain why we were both here in the first place.

My new partner in sex repeated herself, with a trace of impatience this time. "I said I want to get up," she said.

"So get up, already," I said.

"No, you're doing this all wrong," she said, her pink lips pursed into a pout. "You have to say, 'No, you can't get up.'"

"Okay," I said, good sport that I am. "Why don't we just start all over again?"

"Great idea," Maggie said, as if she'd just discovered some new strength in me that she'd overlooked before.

"Now, I want to get up."

"You can't get up." I said. But I could not suppress a giggle.

"Stop laughing," she said.

"I'm sorry, honey, I can't help it," I said and let out a huge guffaw. There is nothing more laugh-provoking than being told you must not laugh. I remember once when my favorite ex-lover and I were hassling about something and my lover's lips were quivering as if she were about to cry. I did not find that funny: I loved the woman. The relationship was important to me. But she said to me, "Now, Nadine, don't you dare laugh!" So of course I burst out laughing. My ex-lover grabbed her pink baby doll pajamas and her copy of *Zami* and went home. She later wrote me a letter to say good bye which was rather cold, I thought. Even now I think we'd still be together if she hadn't asked me not to laugh.

Maggie turned over on her side, with her face towards the wall.

"You're just into vanilla, aren't you?" She sounded dejected.

"Well, I like chocolate ice cream, but I think I prefer vanilla pudding and cookies," I said.

"No, I mean sexually."

"Oh, I try it all." I figured that was safe. I was too insecure to admit I didn't know what she was talking about.

She looked a bit disappointed. Aware that I still owed her an orgasm, I was solicitous. I ran my hand up and down her back and toyed with the space where her bikini panties lay across her voluptuous fanny. "I like tops and sixty-nine," I said, still fishing. I let the panty line go and concentrated on the small v space between her half open legs. "I'm not opposed to dildos either," I continued, "though I don't bother shouting that out at lesbian feminist gatherings." I looked over at her then to see if I was getting close.

I watched her hand inching over towards me. Maggie seemed to have taken the position that the hand was not hers and she had no idea it was crawling up my thigh. "You've never tried any, ah, bondage or leather? Any water sports?" she asked.

Un-huh. I knew what water sports were. "No, I don't think I can handle water sports, but I suppose we can talk about a little bondage or leather." I pride myself on being open minded — just so I'm not the one that gets tied up. I was thinking that dildos were about as kinky as I expected to get, but I wanted Maggie to have her orgasm. So I decided I'd wait and see what I could deal with.

Maggie turned over on her back again. She was smiling now and she even seemed willing to own the hand and the two fingers that were brushing lightly against my pubic hair.

Maggie reached over and grabbed the two lavender ropes tied to each knob of the four poster bed. She put them around her wrists and then motioned to me with her head. I straddled her again and held both her hands down. Maggie ran through her lines again: "I want to get up." she said.

"You can't get up."

"Oh, please! Please! Let me up!" she said. She struggled under me, but could not push me over.

"Let me up," she said again, more urgently this time.

I let her up.

"Why did you do that?" She gave me another disgusted look.

"I thought you really wanted to get up." I said.

"No, no," she said as plaintively as if I'd just made her miss her orgasm. "I want you to hold me down no matter what I say. I like it, Nadine," she said, enunciating slowly as if she were speaking to an addled child. "I really enjoy being held down."

"I feel too guilty when I do that."

"Well, don't feel guilty. Feel guilty because you're interfering with my pleasure by not giving me what I want. Okay?"

"Okay." I was getting a little attitude myself now. Act as if you think I'm dumb and you push my buttons. I pushed her down on the bed and straddled her again. I was about ready to pee on her, too, if she'd asked me to.

"Let me up," she began again.

"You're not getting up," I said, as assertively as I could.

"Oh, please, please, please," she said. To tell you the truth, I think I was beginning to get a little buzz on, too.

"Let me the fuck up," she said.

I hesitated. I don't like being cussed at, particularly when I am making love. Apparently Maggie hadn't picked this up.

"Let me up, slut," she said.

I'd decided I had about had it. I got up off her. I wasn't sure what wired her spark plugs, but this certainly wasn't doing anything for mine. I put my jeans on and stuffed my panties into my pocket.

"Where are you going, Nadine?" she asked in that plaintive voice that meant she knew exactly where I was going and was trying to change my mind.

I leaned over and tied up my shoes without responding.

"I'm sorry, Nadine," she said. "I guess you aren't into humiliation either. My last lover was. I guess I thought . . . " Her words trailed off and stopped.

"I think I'm gonna just split, Maggie," I said. "I know you tried and I tried too, but I'm going home now."

"No, wait," she said. "Couldn't you just give me a spanking first?"

My back was to her and my hand was on the doorknob, when I heard her say, "Could you just tie me up? Give me a few lashes with a small whip or something? Bite me? I could fuck you?"

I was beginning to feel sorry for her. I really was. I turned around to say something to indicate my concern, when I noticed her coming towards me with that chocolate colored dildo centered over that blonde patch of pubic hair. It was bobbing up and down in front of her. "I could fuck you?" she said again.

I tried not to laugh; I swear I did. I mean, there in my mind was poor baby Jesus, wrapped in his blue bunting, wailing his poor little heart out on the floor of that dirty old stable again. But it didn't help.

I tried to blot out the scene of her in that black leather harness with that chocolate colored dildo bouncing up and down. But it was hard (not the dildo, although that was hard, too). What I really mean is that it was difficult not to laugh.

"You're laughing," Maggie said.

"No, I'm not," I lied.

"You are. You're laughing at me, Nadine!"

"I am not," I said with the anger of the guilty.

"Stop laughing!" She said.

"I'm sorry, Maggie." I backed down the hall, laughing and apologizing.

It was most embarrassing.

Not long after that Maggie and I both found the true loves of our lives. But even now, sometimes when I am sitting in on a meeting of the Ashley Baron Advertising Agency, and Maggie will be addressing the staff, standing up there in her tailored black business suit trying to get the staff energized about selling high powered ads, I imagine Maggie's pale body wearing that black harness and that chocolate colored dildo. I get so tickled I have to leave the room.

I'm sorry, Maggie Stevens. I really am.

Kaicha

Connie Panzarino

On the last night of the Michigan Women's Festival, I was lying down in my van feeling depressed about not having met a lover. I debated whether or not to go down to the night stage for the last concert. Some of the women I had met at the Festival came by and asked me to go sit with them. While they were pushing my wheelchair to the concert area, a red haired woman chased me down the hill, shouting, "I'm in love with you! I've read all about you and saw your picture in *Eye to Eye*. I've been going to all your workshops hoping to talk with you, but I chickened out, and I just can't leave Michigan without telling you that I love you and that I want to be with you."

I stopped and smiled. "Why don't you come and sit down with me at the concert? Maybe we can talk." I thought to myself, "This must be some kind of joke." I had been praying to the Goddess about finding a lover here, but this was a little bit much. She sat down on the ground and leaned against my chair. "What's your name?" I asked.

"Kaicha," she replied.

"Where are you from?"

"Oregon."

"Well, I'm from New York." I breathed a sigh of relief because I would probably never see her again.

She smiled, "I know, I'm coming to New York to be with you."

I panicked, but continued talking.

We went for a walk to one of the bonfires and sat for a while talking. "Where did you get the name 'Kaicha'?" I asked. "It's unusual."

"I got it in a Native American circle. It means New Beginnings."

She put her arm around me and was about to kiss me just as a flash of lightning hit very close. It started to rain, and we had to run back to my van. We fumbled with the wheelchair lift in the dark and the rain. When we got into my van, I asked my two attendants to leave us alone for a while. They went off, draped in ponchos. Once again Kaicha leaned forward to kiss me. I closed my eyes in shy anticipation just as two of my friends, Kady and Pagan, opened the van door and pushed in our blind friend, Marge, saying, "Connie, we're gonna leave Marge here for a little while until the storm clears. We'll be right back." Marge couldn't see that I was with someone. I turned red with embarrassment.

After a few seconds of silence, I said, "This is Kaicha. She and I are spending some time in the van." We talked small talk and waited until Kady and Pagan came back for Marge. My attendants came back at the same time.

Kaicha sighed. "I'd better go. I have to check on my son at the boys' camp before the last shuttle. I'll be back in the morning to see you off. I'll need your address so I can come see you next week. I'm coming to New York, and I know you don't believe me, but I am."

She was right, I didn't believe a word of it.

Kaicha did come to New York about two days after we got back. She walked smoothly and a little shyly into my apartment, her eyes wide and blue.

"Do you like lasagna?" I looked up at Kaicha. "I made lasagna."

"Sounds great!"

After dinner, I asked her what she'd like to do that evening.

She said, "I'd like to make love with you."

I thought to myself, "My Goddess, can women really be that direct?" To her I said, "Alright, but I have to do a respiratory treatment first."

My attendant set up my respirator while Kaicha was in the bathroom. I asked her to light a candle and put out the light. Kaicha came out of the bathroom and climbed into bed. She pulled off her shirt and slid under the covers. She had beautiful glistening shoulders from being on the land at Michigan. She watched me as my attendant undressed me in the chair and lifted me onto the bed. My respirator treatment became pleasurable as Kaicha stroked my hair and played with my fingers. When my attendant took my respirator out of my mouth, Kaicha kissed my lips. They were wet from the treatment, and I felt a bit ashamed. "I have a lot of spit after a treatment," I said softly.

"That's good. Sometimes I need a little spit to kind of lubricate things, you know?" She whispered in my ear, and kissed it.

"Mary, you can leave us alone now."

We talked about the hard and the gentle things that happened to us in our lives. We hugged and kissed. We laughed, but even though her lips felt hot and warm on mine, and I wanted to feel them all over me, I felt shy. Kaicha started playing with my hair and sniffing it. I giggled. Then she kissed my fingers one by one, supporting my limp hand in her strong one, and started sniffing again. "What are you doing?" I giggled.

"Getting used to your smells. It takes time to get to know one another. I want to know all of you, but I need to take time. Is that alright?"

"Take all the time you want. It's been a long time for me since I was, you know, with someone."

"Well, maybe we don't have to make love tonight. I mean, what is making love, anyway? I can make love to your hands. I feel like you've made love to me with your eyes already."

Kaicha began to stroke my face lightly with her fingers. She took my hand in hers and moved it gently across her own face. We spent endless time, her touching me, and her moving me to stroke or rub against her. The candle went out and we slept curled up around one another.

The next day we went to the beach, and I sat on her lap in the water. The water ebbed and flowed around us. Because the water made my hands light, I could move them more freely. It was as if there was no gravity to keep them pinned down. I stroked and tickled Kaicha's thighs and she began to touch me between my legs. She stroked my labia and pressed against my clitoris, and held and rocked me in the water till I came. Then she helped me move my hand harder and harder into her in a fast rhythm as we rocked. The waves seemed to get bigger with our orgasms, as the ocean bay made love with us.

The Comet Watchers

Terri L. Jewell

Neither the season nor the time of evening mattered. The six stars in the southern night sky were always there. They pulsed like beads of sweat fixed in a configuration that challenged any connection by a single straight line. The rest of the sky gaped insensately in its blankness. Only the six yellow stars separated the cooling land from the vastness spread above it.

Tinsa and Lonze stood out on their front steps every night to watch the southern sky. Tinsa, known for her beauty in the province, had a large, firm belly and high buttocks that glistened like pearls held between the lips. She was the color of Toudon sand, a deep-well brown that was a step away from the night itself. Tinsa was called upon quite often by the townsfolk to sing the "Century Journeys," poems of the elders from a time before the appearance of the six stars. Lonze, unlike Tinsa, was a restless spirit. She, too, was very dark and had eyes like the pelou fruit whose sour flesh flared a metallic, threatening grey. Both women were quite short in stature, Tinsa being the taller of the two. Lonze was not one to smile easily or trust the townspeople who were always seen crossing over the hills. She trusted no one but Tinsa and was glad for the chilling twilight, the chance to stand quietly next to her Chosen. While Lonze looked out at the stars, she thought that perhaps this night would yield the Sign. The two women stood silently until Tinsa signaled that the time had passed long enough.

During the semi-dark days, the women performed ordinary tasks — fed yatoo grass to their sixteen hooved freelas, prized for their dulcet bleating; mined the hills for singen stones that glowed when cooled to ten keemarks; synthesized the opalescent sheaths that covered them from waists to ankles. Still, each evening without fail, they would stand out on the steps of their small home and watch the sky.

One night after Lonze had stretched her strong legs and arms out of weariness, she noticed the slightest flicker below the third star.

Had she missed it earlier? How long had it been there? Was it too late? Lonze tensed, a sickening sensation leaching through her as she imagined having lost the chance. But when she looked over beside her, she found that Tinsa had closed her eyes and was rocking from side to side gently. Lonze felt a sudden warmth that seemed to leap off Tinsa's body.

"Yes?" Lonze asked.

"Soon," Tinsa whispered. "We had best prepare for that time now."

They were about to go inside when Lonze noticed something out on their land. Lonze lunged down the steps, leaving Tinsa on the porch.

"Move away!" she screamed. "You are much too soon! You all know the legends! Move away!"

She ran out into the stillness, then stopped, heaving from the effort. There were muffled voices, then a mass like some great beast rumbled back toward the direction of town. Lonze looked up for the green flame in the sky once more.

"Yes," she thought. "Yes."

When Lonze returned to the porch, Tinsa was sitting on the stoop. Lonze touched her softly on the head. Tinsa, startled, reached up quickly to clasp Lonze around the wrist. She was trembling.

"Now!" Tinsa whispered harshly.

Without a sound, the two women walked behind the house and up a steep hill. They headed for a dull aqua circle of light that marked the mouth of the mine. They entered the warm, humid passageway. The floor, walls and ceiling were all of the same dense crystal. The tunnel rippled with the glow from the crystal which seemed to oscillate as the women walked through. The passage coursed sharply and the women walked a long distance before Tinsa began to tire. She labored as though the ceiling was bearing down on her, causing her lips to pull back into a grimace.

"Here," Tinsa hissed. "It must be here. It is surely time for me. I cannot go any further. Please."

Lonze froze as if hit with electricity. She smelled the hills and her Chosen standing beside her. She closed her eyes and relaxed. There was an almost imperceivable rush of air over them as they stood expectantly. Then Tinsa turned to face Lonze fully and began to run her fingernail down the length of the sheath covering her belly, her thighs and ankles. Lonze nervously fingered the top of her own sheath. Tinsa's garment slowly opened, then fell away like breath to the floor. The surface of her enormous belly was undulating rhythmically as Lonze gasped at the allurement of it. Yet, it was what was emerging from the delicate, transparent flap of skin under Tinsa's belly that held Lonze spellbound.

Two tiny orange bulbs of flesh were slowly pushing themselves out into the air. They glistened full and moist as the lips of Xanthusian newborns. As they descended on their slender stalk, they throbbed and twitched, pushing out a spiced aroma ahead of them that made Lonze feel unsteady on her feet. Their ropey stem uncoiled systematically, allowing the orange nebulomes to ease further and further down. Tinsa stood expressionless.

As Lonze watched, she began to run her fingernail down the front of her own translucent garment as if pressed by instinct. She pulled in memories of the past when the Sign had boiled in the southern sky and Tinsa's musk seemed to rise off her like smoke. Her wrap fell to the floor and she stepped closer to Tinsa. Lonze felt her nebulomes tense within her as if unsure of their birthing, then ease out of her body. Tinsa's nebulomes had completely extended by this time. The slippery bulbs hung suspended away from Tinsa's body while the stalk writhed in the air weightlessly. Tinsa began to draw in long, deep breaths through her pursed lips.

When the two women were only ten kliparcs apart, their nebulomes began to extend toward one another. Lonze and Tinsa closed their eyes and began to match breathing. Their scents intermingled, making thought and sensation slip away. Lonze began to tremble uncontrollably. She tried to clench her large fists to steady herself, but had no force behind her fingers.

Finally Tinsa's nebulomes touched those of Lonze. At the point of contact, a small green spark flashed. Both women snapped into rigidity. Their breathing ceased, memory and anticipation between them stopped. As the nebulomes flickered rapidly over each other, the passageway in which the women stood was filled with spice and a delicate sucking sound. The viscous surfaces of the inflamed bulbs slid and fluttered over one another excitedly for many hours. The stalks slinked and intertwined in mid-air like crazed salamanders. Lonze and Tinsa stood motionless.

Finally, with their agitation beginning to lessen, the nebulomes began to grind together. Lonze gravitated toward Tinsa as the bulbs and stalk of her nebulomes embedded into the nebulomes of Tinsa. Lonze opened her eyes, and as her body met that of her Chosen, the time of waiting began to come to a close. Tinsa and Lonze initiated

The Comet Watchers

a ritual many, many triltzehs old. Tinsa, with her eyes still closed, opened her mouth. On the very tip of her tongue was a small globe of gold fluid. Lonze felt a rush of warmth in her chest. She parted her lips so that Tinsa could slip her tongue into her mouth. Lonze then closed her lips and began to suck Tinsa's tongue. Lonze felt the ball flatten, then burst, releasing the liquid down her throat.

The dreams arrived instantaneously. She found herself riding freelas on the plains of Mococo, then gliding up the Ulandes peaks where her family, long vaporized, used to live. In these dreams, she learned the ways of the Feared Ones and of prophecy. She continued to suck Tinsa's tongue unconsciously.

The crystal walls of the mine began to pale from their aqua color, then darken. The two sets of nebulomes, suspended and exhausted, began to pull away from one another. As they retracted into the belly-slips, the women backed away from each other. They were not aware of the clear red pool that had spilled onto the floor at their feet. They had seen it many times before and were not alarmed by it. This pool reminded them of the icy red rains in the Choctilian province where there was no dusk or dawn.

When they emerged from the mine, Lonze was in the lead. They found the townspeople kneeling reverently in the yatoo grass. The elders approached and the two women stood aside from the mine, allowing entry of the elders who carried empty flasks. Within a few hours, they re-emerged with their vessels filled with the bright red liquid. They distributed mere drops of it to each person waiting in the fields. Once this was done, they all scurried away anxiously with their elixir to travel back in time to their private dreams of health and wisdom.

Tinsa and Lonze returned home. They nourished themselves on a thick joulapombee stew, then immediately went about their proper chores. And when it grew dark in the southern sky and the six yellow stars glowed their signals into the night, two black-skinned women could be seen standing with their arms about one another to gaze for the next Sign to come for them.

Excerpt from Rocking Bone Hollow

Maureen Brady

    Months passed fleetingly by and brought Marty to the real winter of her long winter. She sat in the rocker and watched the sky change in the late afternoons. The light seemed hopeful; it captured and stole her away from herself the way it came pink before it grayed. It seemed as if her father must have finished decomposing though she hadn't heard a thing about the ashes.
    She'd felt nearly nothing this time when Hester'd said she was going to visit Petra. Yet when the phone call came she was irritated; it interrupted her watching of the sunset.
    "I had a flat," Hester said briskly. "The tire's ruined and I'm afraid to drive all the way home on that little runt of a spare so I'm going to have to stay down here until the morning to get another tire."
    "How did it get ruined?" Marty asked.
    "I didn't realize it was flat and kept driving on it."
    "Oh." How could she, Marty was thinking. How dopey do you have to be to do that? And Hester wasn't dopey. "That's hard to imagine," she said.
    "It was really stupid of me," Hester said.
    Marty wanted to say yes, it sure was, but ended up saying, "Well, don't beat yourself up about it."
    "It was freezing cold or I'd probably have stopped sooner to see why the car was pulling."
    "Yeah," Marty said.
    "I hate to have to sleep here. Petra has a lumpy couch with cat hair all over the place. I'd rather be home with you."
    "Yeah," Marty said again, remembering the sunset. "Well, I'm going now. I'll be at work in the morning but I guess I'll see you later in the day."

She put on mournful music, went back to the rocker and keened at the sky. It was as if her immunity was growing so strong it didn't matter anymore what happened on the outside, as long as she had this part of the day, which she waited for longingly. She rocked and rocked. She wept. And yearned. Occasionally the thought lit a little flare inside her, the charge for a new tire appearing on their Master Card bill. Waste. Hester could have stopped right away and changed it but she liked to put off bad news as long as possible. Marty resented the fact Hester was giving her another resentment. She had no business driving on that tire at my expense, she thought. But she cut off from the flare before it could flame and dropped herself into the music. The pink was nearly gone, the crescent moon was rising. Give me love, she thought, give me love. It was a song, wasn't it? She rocked and keened some more.

After the light was gone she shuffled about the house, thinking of dinner, but she couldn't find anything appetizing to eat so she decided to go to town. She didn't feel wholly herself leaving home, leaving the rocker, but more as if she were sending a representative, someone who was hungry and could not be filled by sunset. She had a vague memory of feeling like this as a child, wanting to send a substitute when her mother would decide to pack them in the car to go out as a search party. She had liked to go to town but not for her mother's purpose — to track down their father and find him clutching to a bar somewhere, telling dirty jokes with strange men who didn't seem like anyone's father, though they often said they were.

She remembered the time in the Yellow Lantern Tavern, Elinore saying, "Okay, let's take that booth and you kids can have a soda. What do you want, coke or ginger ale? And I'll have a cup of coffee, and maybe your father will be embarrassed into deciding to join us." But of course he hadn't. Instead Mrs. Kelly, the fourth grade teacher — Marty had her then, Kate had already had her — came out the door beside the bar that went back to the house part of the building and said hello. And Marty was so embarrassed she wanted to go under the table and nest in the sawdust on the floor. But Mrs. Kelly simply said, "How nice to see you," and didn't let on she knew they'd come to shame their father. She acted as if this was a perfectly normal place for them to stop in for a soda. And when she left Elinore chattered, "Well, wasn't it nice, seeing Mrs. Kelly, did you realize Carl was her husband? She certainly seems fond of you girls. We might as well go now. I guess he'll find his way home on his own sweet time."

But it was only dinner she was searching, Marty remembered, not her father, not Hester; Petra lived an hour away.

Walking down Main Street, she bumped into Sheila, who was out walking her dog. "How's it going?" Sheila asked.

Marty gave her a thumbs down response and Sheila said, "How 'bout a hug?" and hugged her, compressing their two down jackets together tight enough so Marty could feel her body. She thought Sheila uttered a sound, too, not exactly a word but something that seemed empathic, some kind of a wound sound. They weren't exactly friends, only acquaintances who crossed paths now and again. "Where should I eat?" Marty asked Sheila, and Sheila said she'd come along if Marty'd go to O'Neals.

Marty'd never been to O'Neals, which was strange because she'd been around Bridgewater long enough to have been everywhere. It was dark, both from the lighting and the dark wood walls. They took the last booth to get far from the noise of the music. Marty, usually vegetarian, ordered a cheeseburger. "Why the pits?" Sheila asked as soon as the waitress was gone.

"My life's gearing up for a change and yet it feels like I'm standing stark still and can't move. Can't go forward, can't go back."

Sheila nodded. Marty took a deep breath. She felt spacious, as if maybe she'd stepped on top of her father's ghost to say it. She asked Sheila about herself. Sheila said it was the opposite, she couldn't slow it down. "I'm in therapy," she said, "and too much is coming out at once. I can't stop it. I'm like a dry field on fire. I'm trying to deal with incest . . ." She squeezed her eyes closed tight, opened them before she continued. "But I can't talk about my family in therapy yet." She seemed about to jump out of her seat. Then as quickly as she had gotten excited, she sighed and her feelings seemed to drop away from her, and she beamed her focus back on Marty, asking what was going to change.

Marty said she didn't know but talked more openly than she ever had with anyone about her troubles with Hester. Sex was flat, she told her, and she didn't know what happened next. She watched Sheila's face and all the while she talked she felt her attraction to Sheila growing. She watched her prepare to eat her hamburger, small hands quickly darting about the table. Somehow it made her feel good to watch those hands. She remembered the hug, how it had hardly penetrated their coats, yet had comforted her. Sheila's face was small and she grimaced a lot, but when she was relaxed, it looked angelic, as if the cheeks should be touched.

excerpt from *Rocking Bone Hollow*

Marty had taken her boots off and after dinner put her sock feet up on the bench beside Sheila and at one point Sheila grabbed them and pressed them up against her thigh and lust moved through Marty, shaking her, while Sheila went on never losing the beat of the conversation. She remained charged, and lingering there in the booth after the meal was over, she found herself laughing. She found herself saying, "One day I'll look back on this and see it was not as impossible as it seemed."

"What's the it?" Sheila asked.

"Me and Hester, whether we are supposed to go on together or not."

Sheila opened her eyes wider. They were a dark brown and it was dark in the room and Marty tried to but couldn't see into them, they seemed impenetrable. "Heavy," Sheila said, shuddering. "I haven't been in a relationship for several years now because last time I was I lost myself." She shuddered again. "Irv's probably cold," she added.

"Who names a dog Irv?" Marty asked.

"I was trying to get at something about an uncle of mine," she said.

"Did you get it?"

"I don't know you well enough to tell you that I've been known from time to time to kick my dog," Sheila said. "But I'm working on amending my ways."

"Okay," Marty said, "you can expand on that next time we do this, but you're right, Irv's probably cold."

Outside Sheila slipped Irv's leash off the post, petted him and let him lick her face. Then she hugged Marty again. Their coats made a crushing sound but they held tight long enough to push through all the down feathers to contact, and Marty felt a rush and held on a moment longer and Sheila made them sway a little. "Take it easy," she said as they let go of each other. Cupping Marty's cheek with her small hand, she repeated herself, "Take it easy."

Marty couldn't tell if she were blushing or her cheeks were just turning with the cold. "Unexpected as this was," she said, "I'm so glad I found you tonight."

They hugged again, this time more quickly, Marty touching her cheek against Sheila's and registering the soft, downy feel.

* * *

Late afternoons into evenings Marty continued her practice of sitting into sunset. Hester was often not home yet, or she was in the darkroom, or in the kitchen starting dinner, or in her study next door, rolling her desk chair from its place at the desk to the file cabinet. Marty could hear the rasp of its wheels. Hester was orderly. Marty had stacks of papers to file. She always thought if they lived together long enough she'd become like Hester and do it at the end of every day, but she'd never converted. She did it quarterly, with the solstice, or sometimes in between if she got sick.

    She reflected back to that first year when she'd moved in with Hester in the country, giving up her rent-controlled apartment in Greenwich Village as her gesture of true love. (Hester's had been to consolidate and make room for Marty, which she'd done with great generosity.) This had been the part of the day they had almost always shared. Marty, standing at the sink washing lettuce, Hester, coming to embrace her, leaning to kiss her hair, maybe also the nape of her neck, saying, "I love the way your hair is like the bottom of a little heart here." Marty still remembered it well enough to know it must have been extraordinarily lovely to be touched and doted on in that way. Then they'd open the wine and sit down to dinner and encapsulate the happenings of the day. It had seemed, too, oh-so-fullgrown and wholesome of them to allow themselves a fresh bottle of wine each evening.

    Now Marty, more often than not, sat alone sipping sherry, rocking. She didn't like the sweetness but the warmth in her belly felt as if it might be the only thing keeping her alive. Until suddenly, from what seemed like endless time, the signs began to converge to say winter was going to be over. There was a big thaw three days running, which turned the top inch of the road to mud and her snow tires threw big mud splats up on her car. She decided to walk in it, her pants tucked down into her clumsy LL Bean boots, and the smell of the air was suddenly all changed, as if the bark of the trees had opened up pores to imbibe the humidity of the evaporating snow. She pulled the moist air deep into her lungs, thinking maybe now we can get it back, about her and Hester. "What's the it?" she heard Sheila asking, and then she found herself thinking about her instead.

    She went home and called her. "Want to have dinner at O'Neals again soon?" Sheila said yes.

    She took vegetables from the garden out of their freezer, dusted tofu with wheat germ and fried it, and called Hester to dinner. Hester came with her Scotch glass, replenished it before sitting. "Want some?" she asked Marty and Marty hesitated but finally said no. She didn't want to drink so much. She felt it was taking brain cells and dulling

excerpt from *Rocking Bone Hollow*

her mind. Even more than her brain cells, she felt sure it was taking Hester's. It was still voluntary for her, she thought, but for Hester she wasn't sure. She wanted them to quit for a month again as they'd sometimes done before to prove they didn't have a problem.

After dinner Marty said, "Wait, I want to talk," and the words came in a long stream on a run. "Don't you think it's time we stopped being monogamous? Don't you think it might help us if we felt free to open up to others, then we might turn some key that would bring us back together. Not by jealousy, I don't mean that. I mean maybe if we didn't feel obliged to get our sexual satisfaction from this relationship, it would begin to trickle back into us, the desire, the attraction. At least I think so. At least I'd like to try that." She felt like chatterbox Elinore when she realized how long she'd gone on without giving Hester a chance and stopped as abruptly as she'd started.

Hester didn't say anything. "I didn't even realize you'd been thinking about these things," she finally said.

"Of course I have," Marty said. "Sex is a natural human impulse. Nobody goes all that long without thinking about it."

Hester helped herself to more Scotch.

"Well, what do you think of what I said?" Marty asked her.

Hester shrugged. "I guess anything is tryable. But I don't really want it to happen."

"Even if I were to act on it, I doubt I would sleep with anyone who would pose any threat to our relationship," Marty said with a great deal of enthusiasm. She didn't know what she meant by that. She wanted Hester to question her but Hester pushed deep into her chair and dropped her head far back as if she could float herself out to another world. Then she came back to stare at Marty, as if she wanted to will the request out of her.

"I thought we could discuss it," Marty said. "I'm not making unilateral policy. I'm asking what you think about this subject."

"Very little," Hester said. "I wish we could solve it for ourselves." She got up, took her glass, and strode back to her study.

Marty got hot, anticipating her meeting with Sheila as she drove to Bridgewater. They went to the back booth again. Marty took her boots off right away and put her feet up and Sheila rapidly found some excuse to squeeze them affectionately. And Marty was sure they both felt the charge that left her breath short and her speech a little coarse.

"So who was Uncle Irv?" she asked.

"One of the perpetrators, but the nicest one," Sheila answered.

"Oh," Marty said, having reached in deeper than she'd intended to.

They dropped back to easier conversation. Marty could hardly listen. She was too busy asking herself questions. What would it mean if she asked Sheila, "Would you sleep with me?" or declared, "I'm officially non-monogamous now." What would it do to her life? It felt as if she was about to commit a great treachery, but also, if she could turn down the volume on the voices in her head and become only a sensate human, she knew she might feel better than she had the whole year.

After dinner Sheila lifted one of Marty's feet into her lap and began massaging it and Marty struggled not to let anything show in her face. Her legs felt weak with the tingling and she was overtaken with sensation. She nearly had to draw the foot away but breathed deeply instead and left it and let her attention go to the slick, wet feeling below. Sheila put Marty's massaged foot down on the other side of her instead of back where she had got it from so that Marty was straddling her. It was an act of great boldness.

What will she do next, Marty wondered, reach me under the table? She felt ridiculous. This is what people do in bawdy movies, she thought, but she didn't want to lose it, the warmth, the life that had sprung like a fountain. She didn't want winter again. She couldn't begin to admit how she'd suffered each time the sun had gone. She leaned her head against the booth and closed her eyes, taking in the warm buzz, and Sheila ran her hands up the side of Marty's legs, softly and only to the knees but it forebode more to come and they both knew it. And Marty kept her eyes closed but let a little gasp escape her mouth. She felt as if she might come right there in the booth without anything that officially resembled love making. She turned her arches in and ran her feet down Sheila's thighs and Sheila smiled, both devilish and soft, opened her legs a little and brought one of Marty's feet to her crotch. Just then the waitress came to clear the table and Marty pulled the foot away, down to the floor.

She ordered another beer. Sheila ordered Sleepytime tea. Marty felt they'd come close to being reprimanded, though by whom she didn't know. The waitress seemed oblivious. She waited a minute but when the waitress didn't return, she put her foot back where Sheila had placed it and pressed her heel into Sheila and felt how hot she was. Sheila pulled on her toes playfully. "This little piggy,

excerpt from *Rocking Bone Hollow*

that little piggy." They had long since stopped trying to keep up conversation. The waitress came back. Marty left her foot in Sheila's lap. Give me love, she mused and then thought how fast decadence slides into feeling like normal.

When they finished the drinks, Sheila asked, "Want to come back to my place?" Marty looked hard at her for a minute, again noticing how she couldn't see into her eyes, couldn't see light in them. "I do," she said, "but I don't think I ought to. Too confused," she gulped over the words.

Sheila sighed and shrugged. "Suit yourself."

Marty said, "I'm sorry. I wish I weren't so conflicted."

Driving home she regretted having passed it up. She tried to get back the tingling glow, the feeling of life waking up in her center, where she had felt so dried up and low. You're afraid of it, afraid of anything too lively, she accused herself, then took the other side. What of you and Hester, could you do this without a severance of your bond? In her head she had worked it out as if that were possible. In the rest of her body she didn't know. She sensed it would be a knife slicing them clean apart, like a pear cut in two.

The best person I've ever had, she thought of Hester. She was so loyal and devoted to me from that first day. And we were able to be quiet together, cheer each other's work, grunt over a bad mood at the breakfast table, and build ourselves a home. She flashed on a frame of Hester holding the sheetrock in place while she hammered. "Go for it, Marty, this is no light mass, go for speed, not precision." Still, she was a solid block, knowing Marty was only equipped to rush so much.

She regretted they'd quit therapy, though not that particular therapist Amanda, who'd been too easily manipulated by Hester. She'd asked what was the problem? Marty'd said, "Anger, we need to learn how to fight with each other." Hester'd said confident, "I think I know when you're angry." "What does she do?" Amanda'd asked. "She goes quiet," Hester replied. "What does Hester do?" she'd asked Marty. "Either gets depressed or goes out and backs the car into walls or posts or ditches." Amanda had laughed, agreeing in a backhand way with Hester that this wasn't the problem. But understanding what the other did didn't mean they knew how to take it through. But Marty was too angry by then and went silent, just as Hester had described she might instead of saying, "You missed the point, both of you."

Getting into bed with Hester that night, she looked hard at her, as if she were taking in a new view through a secret. Hester didn't mind, she was asleep already. Marty was propped against the headboard, reading. She held a hand on Hester's head. Precious, she kept thinking, so precious, and then she felt a slight crack open in her heart.

It was another two months before she took up with Sheila. It had to do with the weather getting warm, the ground getting fragrant. It had to do with her opening the window in her study, taking off the storm windows, and the owl cooing up over the hill, which seemed to call her. It had to do with the spring green growing more lush every day until she was about to explode with watching it.

She called her. It wouldn't have surprised her if she had blown her chances. In a way she hoped she had. But Sheila said, "Yes, I'd love to go on a hike to a place you know where there's a wonderful waterfall and no one ever goes there."

She picked her up in Bridgewater. "What about Irv?" Sheila asked.

"It's up to you." Marty remembered her calling Irv perpetrator. "Maybe you'd like to leave him home."

"It would be a real treat for Irv, but fuck it," she said. "I don't feel like dealing." She closed Irv in the apartment and he whimpered but they walked away.

Sheila looked ridiculous, Marty thought, like a Girl Scout in khaki shorts and hiking boots. The canvas thermos she carried had the appearance of World War II surplus. She walked with a bouncy energy; she seemed like a kid. Still, when they bumped, there were sparks abounding.

They drove an hour, then walked for two, and by the time they reached the waterfall, Marty felt more like a child herself. The water sparkled, the sky was like a ceiling, and the leaves shimmered in the wind. She lay on her back on a large, flat rock, warm because it had absorbed the sun, and felt how she too could absorb it. She closed her eyes and breathed deep. Hester, Hester, Hester, she thought, as if she were already a memory. How I have loved you. She felt that crack in her heart again and a tear came with it and then she returned to the feeling of the sun.

Sheila was face down at the edge of the rock, looking into the pool of water. Marty went beside her. She wanted to be responsible for initiating this. She looked down into the water with her. "How do you like it?" she asked.

excerpt from *Rocking Bone Hollow*

"I like it fine," Sheila said. "I feel like a kid come out to play."

Marty put her arm across Sheila's back and pulled herself close to her side. Still looking down to the water, she felt the wave of lust ripple through her. Sheila uttered a little noise, maybe the wound sound again. Marty ran her hand down Sheila's back and rested it on her buttocks and felt the quiver of a muscle going taut. She could hear her own breath. She could hear Sheila's, too. She could hear birds and always the water, which coursed over the rocks above and landed in a roar on the other side of the pool.

Marty turned over and sat up, legs out in front of her. Sheila came and sat opposite her, legs out in a V. She methodically untied Marty's double bows and removed her sneakers, then pressed both heels into her crotch the way she had in the restaurant. She leaned forward and ran her hands up Marty's legs to her hips, then ran them over to the insides of her thighs. Marty let her head loll back as she murmured and Sheila stayed there, brazen, pressing a thumb into the seam of Marty's jeans. Marty leaned back. It was tight in her chest but she could still feel the sun.

She reached Sheila's foot and brought it closer. "Let's take this ridiculous boot off," she said, but Sheila moved it away.

"No, I like it. I want to be the butch with the boots. I've never done it quite this way before."

"What way?" Marty asked, rubbing her own breasts provocatively in spite of the innocence in her voice.

"I'll tell you more later," Sheila said, running back down the length of Marty's legs again, then pulling her to bend her knees. "Come closer."

Marty did. Sheila's legs cradled her. She bent forward and they kissed. It was a kiss full of urgency. Sheila's tongue entered and searched her, then when she penetrated Sheila, Sheila pulled her tongue in deeper, too hard. It hurt her. When had she and Hester stopped tongue kissing? The thought flew by her like a bird which would light on a branch out of vision and be forgotten. After the kiss she tried to hug Sheila but Sheila pushed her back, hand on the middle of her chest, saying, "Relax, I want you. I want to do you. And I don't want you to worry about me."

"Why not?" Marty said.

"Because this is my pleasure," Sheila said.

Marty was embarrassed but couldn't really object. It had been her fantasy, hadn't it? Her body said yes. Her body was alive and wanting.

Sheila had opened her jeans. She'd gotten one of those small hands down inside there and a finger or two inside Marty. Marty felt taken. It was what she had wanted. She had wanted it from Hester. Her back was on the rock. Sheila was shaking her. Had a hand inside her and was pumping her with life. She had the other hand on Marty's breast under her shirt. She moved it from one to the other. She pulled her nipples and Marty felt the pull in her vagina.

"You sure we're safely alone?" Sheila interrupted.

Marty opened her eyes. She stared at the incredible green and the sky and then at Sheila's dark eyes, maybe the pupils were dilated, maybe that's why they still couldn't be seen into. Then she saw herself, a woman laying on a rock, panting, on fire. The committee in her head would be quick to judge her but she could stand up for the fact there was something that felt honest about what she was doing.

She smiled boldly at Sheila. "Pretty sure."

"Let's get these jeans at least part way down then," Sheila said, as if it were merely a practical statement.

Sheila came out of Marty to pull the pants down over her butt and it gave Marty a moment to feel herself separate again. She watched the pants going down, underwear with them. She saw her pubic hair sparkling with moisture. Sheila ran a hand down through it and back up her belly to display the wet proudly. She lifted Marty's bottom up onto her leg. Then she had her again. She went in. She probed. She tried different fingers. She had the nipple again, the other breast pegged with her forearm. She made little noises. She rocked her leg under Marty. Marty moaned openly. She followed Sheila's hand with her moans. She didn't know where else this could go, but Sheila took one of the slick fingers out of her vagina and slid it in her ass. She had her now everywhere. She was taken. Shaken at the root. She cried out. She felt full. It was hard for her to breathe. She grew frightened someone would come upon them, she had better hurry up. But still she was languid. She didn't want it to be over. She feared she'd go back to where she'd come from, the flimsy feel of returning to dust.

Sheila moved in her deeply and she gasped. "Ah, she likes it," Sheila said, entering and entering. "You are wonderful beyond my wildest imagines," she said. Marty couldn't imagine that Sheila had an imagination, she seemed to act everything out. She couldn't imagine what she was doing there with her. This was not like her. She considered herself moderate, modest, shy. But she was there, undeniably. Sheila's fingers had entered her mouth and she was sucking them, restraining herself from biting them, and Sheila was plunging, then pulling back, then plunging again in all her orifices. Marty surrendered to it and Sheila got hotter, breathless, though her hands still moved coolly, as if she were an orchestra conductor, synchronizing the pulses that beat in both of them. And then Marty rushed like the water over the fall. She felt as if she were drooping further down on the rock, almost falling backwards, and then she was the pool, and Sheila held still though she remained deep inside her, and the sun was shining at an angle that beamed its rays upon her upturned center, and she could tell Sheila was smiling, even before she looked to see.

* * *

The walk back passed quickly. When they got to the car, Sheila, sideways, inclined her head against the seat and looked again like a child. "I haven't had so much fresh air in an eon," she murmured. It was hard to believe she was the same one as the butch with the boots.

Marty took up the small hand and squeezed it. "I don't know what this is. I don't know who I am today, much less you," she said.

Sheila's vulnerability flickered, then vanished. "You were one hot mama and I was up for it," she crowed.

Marty's face colored and she disliked Sheila for putting it that way, especially at that moment. She was so without foundation, her faithfulness to Hester so recently severed, that anything but humiliation would go better with her freedom.

She made the dizzying drive down through the mountains. Each curve was treacherous, too banked, too serious; granite straight down gaped, taking her breath as Sheila had. She remembered her father driving them as kids through the mountains and how she'd loll her head, letting it roll with the curves until a refrain would come speaking to her from the tires, repeating over and over. She let herself go to the rhythm of the turning, right curve, left curve, listen to the tires. The rhythm was quieting but the message was not. Whose are you now? Whose are you now? was what the tires said.

Invisible Lines

Tee A. Corinne

Start with the sex. Not the long slow romantic build-up but the hot, rhythmic, cunt-in-the-face kind of sex, sixty-nining it through the air-conditioned afternoon, on and on in the rocking, moaning, sloshing around of good sex, coupled with familiarity.

Start with the sex, although the relationship didn't start with the sex unless you count the wild intellectual excitement, ideas intertwined, the intimacy of long talks late into the night.

Who would have thought I would come to crave her body like I do?

It didn't start with sex, but sensual pleasures were always there, near, just under the surface. She brought me carrots, huge, fresh from her garden, sliced crosswise into disks through which the sun glowed like stained glass. I would bite into them, sucking the juice from the layers, holding them against my lips, sliding so easily into her conversation that I didn't notice when I crossed the invisible line, when I couldn't imagine not having her in my life.

What is the need of one person for another? Where did I admit that my need for her included a physical component? I ate her food. We talked.

She brought me freshly roasted almonds which she pronounced with a hard "a," laughing about her childhood in almond country, apricot country where the oak leaves are a deep bluegreen and the snowcapped mountains are a constant presence.

As we ate and talked, the leaves around us whispered words I could almost understand, sang me songs I could almost remember. Distant mountains humped in womanly curves.

We sat side by side, together. Heat filled my nostrils. She ate slowly, talking between bites. As she talked she gestured. I noticed that her hands were square.

There are ways that autumn sunlight refracts off red-gold madrone, through white oak and black oak and big-leafed maple. Light filled the glen in which we sat on the small, graceful bench. Light seemed to fill me, to feed me, as did the stories we shared, the flowers she brought, the crinkly, crunchy hearts of lettuce from her garden.

There was a long courtship, a slow coming together, the incest in my past a buoy to be navigated, a fact to be acknowledged, territory needing to be charted and defused.

She waits whenever I need her to.

Gratitude and pleasure mix elegantly.

Although it didn't start with sex, I was intensely aware of her body, her physical presence in my life. She's hard not to notice: radiantly healthy, quick and easy with the turn of a phrase, joking about being a redneck intellectual.

She knows the ordinary names of more trees than I do, knows the Latin names as well. Her respect for the land is warm, full of listening, communication. She listens to me like that, listens to what I say and to how my body moves. Sometimes I think of her as a gift, part of my survival, of my healing.

Where does sex start? Where does it stop? Of what is it composed?

I rest holding her backside against my stomach, my hand cradling her breast, holding onto it, steering by it, its form just right for my hand. Her areola is smooth and intense under my fingers as I stroke and rub.

She laughs that I come, sometimes, from the excitement of touching her, the feel of her silken nipples, shy, delicate, voluptuous.

It took us so long to touch for the first time.

We touched for so long once we began.

We touch now, frequently, sometimes lightly, yet never casually, never without meaning.

And sometimes sex, the specifics of genital sex, enfolds us. I bury my face, you know, in that warm and fragrant place between her legs, and lose my self in the conversations of desire, of my body and hers saying, "Here," "Now," "This," "I want," "I want you."

Sex binds.

Across the Straits of Georgia

Amanda Hayman

I was glad the weather had stayed fine for my ferry ride back to the mainland. Every morning as I'd looked out of the tent, I'd held my breath, in case the marvelous clear sky I'd become accustomed to should have been traded for one promising rain. Now the burning sun heightened the colours to a heart-breaking intensity, and I admired my own dark tan and dazzling white tank top no less than the fabulous array of blues; navy and turquoise for the sea, periwinkle above me. This time yesterday I'd been dreaming on the little dock that abutted the campsite, trailing my toes in this same salt water.

Idly I turned my attention to the people emerging in a steady stream from the stairwell behind me. Although I'd been far from the first to arrive at the Schwartz Bay ferry compound, my car had been directed by some lucky chance to the line which would be selected first for boarding. Everyone looked tanned and relaxed, blinking in the sunlight and flashing white teeth and matching shorts as they argued and laughed with friends or spouses about the best location from which to enjoy the ninety-minute trip. There were loads of children, too, skittering backwards and forwards in the lurid fluorescent beachwear that seemed to be all the rage, rivalling the noisy seagulls in their bids for attention. I couldn't understand why anyone would want to be inside on a morning like this, despite the lure of the $8.75 brunch buffet that was being announced over the p.a., but many of these holiday-makers lingered to glance over the railing for only a minute before moving on, leaving my sun-drenched spot uncrowded.

As a dark head came within my line of vision, idle curiosity changed to rapt attention. Always on the lookout for dykes, I'd marked one woman as a candidate when everyone was hanging about waiting to drive on board, and here she was again. Of medium height, stocky, with fluffy black hair standing up pertly at the crown, a lazy confidence oozing from her lengthy stride and swinging hips. Oversized sunglasses obscured the top half of her face, but I judged her to be in her early forties, a few years younger than myself.

Surreptitiously I nudged my own sunglasses from the top of my head back over my eyes, and assumed what I hoped was a nonchalant stance. She stopped for a moment, glancing up and down the deck, as if trying to make a decision, then turned and sauntered in my direction.

I suppose that if we hadn't both been wearing dark glasses our eyes might have met, but as it was, we exchanged a casual "Hi," and that brief smile of recognition that says, "I know you know."

For a moment I watched the space where she had been, wondering vaguely whether I should be feeling guilty about admiring the curves of a perfect stranger's body. Then I turned away in a hurry — supposing she came out and caught me staring like a fool? In any case, the ship had started moving, and the delectable vistas of the southern Gulf Islands were spread out before me like some superior technicolour postcard. Spangles of light skipped up and down the surface of the water, and the sharp smell of salt tantalised my nostrils. The metal of the railing was hot against my forearms, and I began to enter the dreamy trance that sun on the back of my neck always brings on. The image of the dark-haired woman receded to the edges of my consciousness. Yep, if I had to go back to Vancouver and the familiar old work routine, this was a fine way of doing it.

As the ship chugged smoothly around tiny Moresby Island, I became aware of someone standing behind my left shoulder. I turned a little, preparing to be irritated by this intrusion into my reverie, and found myself looking at a pair of large sunglasses and a cheerful grin.

"Hi." It was that woman, holding out a bag. "Have a crisp."

"Thanks." I took a chip, wondering at the unfamiliar word. We stood side by side, companionably munching.

"These islands are fantastic," my new friend enthused. "So green and lush. I wonder if it's possible to stay on any of them." The clipped accent and long vowels needed close attention if I wasn't going to miss anything.

"I've been camping on Saltspring this week — that's the biggest island, you know." I wished she'd take off those glasses so I could see her eyes. "There are some bed and breakfast places there, too. I don't expect they're expensive; well, more than camping, of course, but not like the big hotels. I think you can stay on just about all the islands. It's a seasonal thing, but you could ask at the tourist office in Vancouver." I was babbling, I knew, but the proximity of her tanned shoulder to my own bare arm was tantalizing, and I needed to distract myself from the unexpected acrobatics in my stomach.

With a flourish she swept off her sunglasses and held out a hand. "Maybe I will. My name's Denise, by the way."

"I'm Kat. Well, Katrina, really, but my friends all call me Kat." Her eyes were dark brown, very soft, a golden ring around the iris. As she moved I caught the mingling odours of sweat and musk. She wore a loose, open weave cotton top in a warm pink that seemed to glow against the rosy tan of her exposed arms and throat.

"Hi, Kat," she said simply, then put back her glasses and craned her head to watch a flock of seagulls flying overhead in precise formation.

The day, which had moments before been merely beautiful, assumed a crystalline quality. The outlines of the trees etched themselves in sharp relief against the matte azure canvas of the sky, whilst the midday sun, suddenly ten times stronger, laced the sprinkling of yachts we were passing with festoons of liquid silver. I smiled to myself, and knew I was happy.

"Where are you from?" My tongue seemed to have magically untangled itself.

"England."

"What part?"

"I live in Coventry now." Denise waited, but seeing no signs of recognition cross my face, went on. "In the Midlands. Near Birmingham?"

"Oh, yeah." I'd look at the atlas when I got home. "What brings you to Canada?" I asked.

"Oh, I've been working in Montreal for nearly a year." She motioned to the lifebelt container behind us. "Let's sit down."

We settled ourselves, still as close, I noticed, as we had been when hanging over the railing.

Denise continued. "I'm a primary school teacher, and when the possibility of an exchange came up, I jumped at the chance."

"And how do you like it?" I'd often wondered about working abroad myself.

"Well, it's over now, I'm taking some time to travel before I go home, but it's been a fantastic experience. The teachers I've been working with are so willing to experiment with new ideas, I'm just dying to try out some of the things I've learnt with our pupils." She ran her fingers through the short hair on her crown, causing it to stand up even more than before. "What about you, Kat?"

"I'm a teacher, too." Surely not a coincidence that we had this much in common.

"Oh, really. What do you teach?"

"English as a second language, to Asian immigrants."

"Do you like it?"

I nodded. "Yes, I do. The students are very anxious to acclimatise to their new life in Canada, and I feel that in many cases I'm a major link to the culture of my country."

"Oh, you're a Canadian, are you? Sorry, I never can tell from the accent." She touched my forearm lightly, by way of apology. Was it my imagination, or did her fingers linger just a second longer than was necessary? I glanced at my arm, almost expecting to see her fingerprints seared across my skin, but nothing was visible. Just as I had to assume that the heart thumping in my ears was audible to me alone.

For a few minutes we sat listening to the shipboard bustle and the steady swishing as the ship cleaved its path through the water. Somehow the few centimetres between our thighs had disappeared, and as I leaned backwards, one of the hands supporting me rested close to the small of her back. I studied her profile, the long face with its delicate snub nose, and wide-lipped mouth. I wondered what it would be like to kiss her, and instantly knew that I very much wanted to do so. If I moved my hand ever so slightly I would be able to caress her back. I sighed.

"What's that for?" asked Denise, pressing her thigh into more deliberate contact with mine.

"Oh, nothing." I wasn't ready to be blatant. "How long did you stay on Vancouver Island?"

The corners of her mouth lifted before she replied, as if aware of my ruse. "Six nights. I rented a car in Vancouver, then took the ferry to Nanaimo. After that I drove over the mountains to the west coast of the island. I wanted to see the Pacific Rim National Park—there were some dykes in Montreal who raved about it. Have you been there?"

I shook my head and laughed. "You know how it is, you never see your own country."

"I do. You'll probably be shocked to know that I've never been to Scotland."

I laughed again. "That's one of the first places Canadians make for when they go to Europe. So tell me about this national park."

"Miles and miles of beach." She threw out her arms. "And completely unspoilt. I walked for three hours one day, and hardly saw a soul. Imagine that! In August, too!"

"Do you like travelling on your own?"

"Mmm, for me it's the best way to go. But," her voice dropped, "I also like very much to be with another woman."

What was there to say to that? My cheeks started to tingle, and I knew I was blushing.

By now we were out in the open sea, leaving behind the domestic coziness of the islands. The vastness of the water was in front of us, stretching almost to the horizon, where a faint edge of land was visible. I knew this meant that in thirty-five minutes we'd be at Tsawassen, and said so.

"So you've done this crossing before?" Denise was intrigued.

"Yeah, lots of times. I don't get long holidays, like schoolteachers, but a week off here and there. This ferry is one of the fastest ways out of the city, and the islands have marvelous weather."

"And you spend all your time in the sun, right?" Denise hoisted the straw basket she had dropped by our feet and rummaged for a moment. Her feet were dirty and rather large, thrust into a pair of the cheap, brightly-coloured plastic sandals that were so popular that summer.

I caught sight of a familiar cassette box in her basket.

"They're great, aren't they?" I pointed downward.

"Who? Oh, Ova, you mean?" Her gaze followed my finger.

"Yeah, I've got a couple of their tapes, but I've never seen them live."

"Oh, that's too bad. I saw them in London a few years ago, and I couldn't take my eyes off the stage the whole two hours they were playing." Denise swung her legs so they banged against the side of the lifebelt container. "I mean, you get the feeling that they believe in what they're singing about."

"Yes, that's just how I feel!" Not too many of my Vancouver friends were familiar with this music, so I hadn't talked much about it before, except to encourage them to borrow my cassettes. "When I listen to the words I feel, well, as if there *is* a point in trying to change things, maybe I can make a difference. Probably that sounds stupid." I'd never tried to put these ideas into words before, after all.

"No, it's OK, I understand." Denise squeezed my hand. "I get inspired when I listen to that tape, too."

"I suppose it's because they're British." I said.

She laughed. "I don't expect that's all it is. And anyway, one of them's Canadian, you know."

"Really?" I felt pleased out of proportion.

Now Denise resumed her search in the straw basket, and after a minute she held out a tube. "Your neck's burning," she said in a matter-of-fact tone.

I squeezed out the fragrant cream and slathered it on my neck and shoulders.

"Don't forget the ears," reminded Denise.

"How about you?" I held out the lotion.

"Well, if you wouldn't mind, I think my back could do with some." She turned sideways, and wriggled her shoulders in invitation.

Her skin was warm and incredibly soft. I took my time, anointing all the areas of exposed skin within my reach. I pulled down the strings that formed the straps of the pink top to avoid getting cream on them, marvelling at the curve of her shoulders. The nape of her neck, covered by feathery wisps of the dark hair, looked fragile; it was all I could do not to pull her backwards so that she would lean against my breasts, but given our surroundings, I resisted.

"Thanks." She took back the tube. "What about your face?"

"Oh, no problem, it's past getting burnt." I smiled, remembering my million freckles.

"Well," her voice was husky, "At least take off those sunglasses, so I can see your eyes." So saying, she dropped her own glasses into the straw bag.

Awkwardly, I complied with her request, meeting her unshielded gaze.

"Nice," she said, and put up a hand to brush back a strand of my hair. A hand that was, I noticed, a little unsteady in its movements. For the first time I dared to think past the end of the ferry journey. Where was all this leading?

A couple of teenagers went by, talking about the mountains they'd seen from the other side of the ship. Denise looked at me.

"Want to go and look?"

"Sure."

I led the way through the darkness of the crowded lounge, to the shadowy side of the ship. It was much colder here, and the mountain-viewers pressed themselves to the hull for protection against the wind. But you could see the mountains.

We stood as close together as we could get, gazing at the snow-capped peaks, soaring out of the mist ahead like a froth of crisply-starched linen.

"Wow," breathed Denise. "Wow. What a glorious sight."

"I'm glad you like them," I said shyly, as if I'd laid on the show especially for her enjoyment. "I think they're at their best seen from the ferry."

"I'd love to go there, but I suppose it'll have to wait 'til next time."

I took a deep breath. "How long will you be in Vancouver?" I asked, wanting to add, "And would you like to stay with me?"

"Ah, I thought you might ask that." She put an arm round my waist, and leant her head against my shoulder. We were the same height, and fitted well together.

When she didn't reply, I asked again, "How long?"

"The thing is, I've cut it as fine as I dare already." She sighed deeply. "I'm flying out of Seattle tonight."

"Where to?" The mist over the coastline seemed to be coming this way.

"To London."

I stiffened. "Really?"

"I'm afraid so," and from the sadness in her soft brown eyes I knew she really was sorry.

I looked at my watch. It was nearly 12:30. "What time is your flight? How long will it take to drive to Seattle?" Somewhere I was hoping that time could be made for a breathless dash to my apartment before she had to leave.

"To the airport? Oh, three or four hours. My flight's at 6:45."

"Can't you change it?"

She shook her head. "Oh, Kat, I wish I could. But it was a cheap ticket, and this is the last day it's valid."

Oblivious to the people milling around us, she took my face between her hands. I could see the pulse beating at the base of her throat, felt her breath on my cheek. Then we were hugging each other for all we were worth. Warmth rose inside me, the insistent snake uncoiling for Denise, refusing to accept the imminence of her departure.

"Will all passengers please return to their vehicles and prepare for arrival at Tsawassen." The impersonal voice sliced through our embrace. Our cars were in separate parts of the ship, we discovered, and we had no way of knowing in which order they'd unload the ferry. For a few minutes more we clung to each other, then hastily searched for scraps of paper to exchange addresses, knowing as we did so that we would never use them. It was now or never. A year into the future, or ten, we would be changed, our meeting awkward as we found ourselves unable to recapture the brilliance of our attraction.

We could linger no longer, the quay was hovering to the side of the ship, and the foot passengers were hurrying to the front of the vessel, eager to disembark. Denise kissed me on the mouth with a suddenness and intensity that made me want to cry.

Then she was gone, that same long stride, but this time departing, leaving me to find my way to my car with unshed tears in my eyes. The taste of her still in my mouth, I followed the stream of cars driving off the boat.

White Chocolate

Natalie Devora

Have you ever tasted
White Chocolate?
Soft and sensual
A delight to the tongue
Sweeter than the ripest strawberry
Juicier than the peach that drips
into your mouth on a hot day
Downright tasty.

Have you ever dipped your fingers
into the creamy sensation
White Chocolate?
Felt it cling
Teasingly
Causing those fingers to proceed
Directly to your mouth
Just for a little taste
Really.

Don't you want to taste,
Dip your fingers into
Surround your tongue with
Wrap your lips around some
White Chocolate?

Come on
You truly might like it
Might not ever want to stop
I know you've shied away before
Feast upon me
White Chocolate.

Natalie Devora

The following speech was delivered at the Disability and Sexuality Panel, OUTWRITE '91, San Francisco, CA, March, 1991.

The piece "White Chocolate" emerged one evening out of my need to define my identity as an African-American Albino lesbian. I needed to show my sisters with luscious brown skin that I, too, was/am chocolate, not of brown hue, yet chocolate nonetheless. I was frustrated by hearing poems that spoke of the richness of pigmented skin, brown, caramel, sepia, coffee, honey — color I did not have. I felt inferior because of my white skin. I felt less Black. I felt invisible.

I want to talk about invisibility. I am here at this conference and still I am invisible. How many of you know that I cannot see detail from more than ten feet away? How many of you would even understand that this conference is a disability nightmare for me? I mean there are nearly two thousand people here. Unless I happen to be directly in your face I am not going to see you. Yet do I appear or look disabled? I do not carry any definable instrument, white cane or guide dog, to define myself. I am not totally blind. I fall into the nebulous category of being legally blind. A title that doesn't really define anything.

Last night I was here for the keynote speeches. I had to ask about accessible seating reserved for people with disabilities. I could see none. I had to, yet one more time, assert myself in order to be able to see. I later learned from one of the conference organizers that seats had been reserved in the front row for disabled people. I was angry because I felt that non-disabled people had taken seating made available to me and others with disabilities. I was angry because, yet again, ableism prevented someone with a disability from having access. I want to ask that when we have our conferences and gatherings we create seating for people with disabilities automatically. I also want to state that accessibility does not end with wheelchairs and interpreters for the deaf and hard of hearing. I am asking that we look beyond the visible disability to recognize the invisible.

I have seen no images of myself in lesbian erotica nor have I seen myself depicted in writings of/about/on disability. I have become my own spokesperson. I stand before you today tired of speaking out for myself. Yet I continue to speak out because I hope that just maybe by my risk-taking to write my story, another Albino child ten years from now will have something to read and won't have to forge the way.

I began writing erotica nearly three years ago. I began to write because I was bored with most of the lesbian erotica that I did encounter. I wanted to read about more than women stroking other women's honey pots and women's wetness. I wanted to read about pussies and cunts. I wanted to read more than five paragraphs in two hundred pages about women making love. I wanted to read about women fucking. I am not saying that to write about soft and gentle lovemaking is not to be done. I am saying that I wanted and needed more from the erotica that was being published.

I was forced, then, to put my fantasies down on paper. For me this did not mean that my words were to be heard by other women, not at that point. Before I was to ever read publicly my erotica or submit any short story for publication, I had to overcome a few hurdles. I had to do a lot of healing. Being an incest survivor caused me to hate my body. I hated my body for being violated. I hated my body for responding to my perpetrator's touch. I hated my body for betraying me. I had to learn that I was beautiful. For me beauty was associated with color. This association was ingrained in my brain by my mother who never ceased to compare me to my lovely sister who had beautiful light brown skin. This ingrained association was what caused me to dye my hair, from the time I was thirteen until I left home at eighteen, because my mother believed that this would give me greater acceptance.

I had to discover that I liked sex. That may sound strange, but I carried a tremendous amount of guilt for enjoying the sensations that my body gave me. So I became a closet Eroticist. I bought and read everything I could get my hands on that was erotic. Be the material good or bad, I read it. I was even forced to read mainstream erotica. It wasn't until three and a half years ago when I fell in love with a gorgeous Black woman that I began to write erotica. This woman taught me about romance. She taught me that I was capable of being loved. With her I danced my very first slow dance. With her my Blackness was an accepted fact, a natural part of my identity. With her I had incredible, extremely satisfying sex.

I wrote a short story entitled "The Tryst." She was the inspiration for that piece. For she was my first and finest mistress. "The Tryst" is a fine piece of writing, one that will leave the reader with wet underwear, but what "The Tryst" fails to mention is that both characters are disabled women. The story doesn't talk about having sex with a woman who uses a wheelchair, nor does the story tell of a woman who has never seen her own cunt. The characters remain able bodied.

I did not feel comfortable writing about disability and sexuality. I felt too vulnerable and exposed. For me it has been easier to simply write about women being spanked. It has been easier to write about my muscled soft butch lover sitting atop my cock, not dildo but cock. I can focus on what is seemingly easier while avoiding the more personal.

When I did begin to think about how my disability related to my sexuality, I thought about all the things that I'd never done because of my albinism. Those things include:

never having gone cruising in a bar
never having picked up or been picked up by anyone in a bar
never openly flirted across a room
never having had sex on the beach during the day
never having seen the intricacies of my pussy
never having seen the true color of my eyes
never having done anything naked in the sun
never having driven a car

I then began to think of the things I have done because of my Albinism:

I have come to appreciate the goodness of the sun despite my sensitivity to it.
I have been an ophthalmological guinea pig
I dyed my hair and passed for white
I have been subject to ignorant ridicule and stereotypes
I have been assumed asexual
I have been teased for looking different
I have had all thirty one flavors at 31 Flavors read to me because they were listed on a wall
I have learned to memorize my lover's body through touch

These things are all important because they are a part of my personal make-up. They are a part of my history.

I don't think about all of these things on a day-to-day basis. If I did I would continually be depressed because I was/am oppressed. However, I am continually reminded of my differentness each time I leave the sanctuary of my apartment. I am subject to racism. I get it from the people that I work with for being the only African-American person at the company, because most of them don't bother or want to let my ethnicity penetrate their brains. I feel the ostracism from other Blacks, gay and straight, because I make them uncomfortable, either for being a lesbian or for being a white-skinned Black woman in this society. I exist caught oftentimes between worlds, on a fence with no name. I straddle it hungering for acceptance. I long to be embraced by my people.

Today I am asking all of you to examine your shortcomings. How many times have you looked away from a Black woman or man because of their color? How many times have you crossed to the other side of the street out of fear? How many times have you turned away in embarrassment at the sight of a severely disabled person? How many of you have been physically attracted to a person with a disability? Who amongst you has had a sexual encounter or relationship with a disabled person? How many of you are guilty for holding community events in an inaccessible location? We are all guilty of these transgressions. I am no exception. I am asking that we all stop, today, to look at ourselves. I am asking that we all begin to bridge a gap. I am asking that we all take a risk.

Friends

Chea Villanueva

It had been getting dark in the studio for a while. The canvases stacked in the corner were an indistinguishable sculpture. Toward the west side of the city you could still see the lavender and orange streaks of sunlight reflected through the windows. It had been a hot oppressive day and was turning into an equally oppressive night. The heat was rising lazily off the street. Even though it was early evening when most New Yorkers were usually heading for dinner and entertainment, no one was rushing on the street below. The old vendor man on the corner packed up his fruit and vegetables; kids on roller skates gave up the race. And still we sat.

We had known each other for a long time. I wasn't sure of how many years. She kept track of things like that. Long enough to cry together, laugh together, and dream together; which is enough to make any two people friends. The ice had melted in our wine coolers. Neither of us made a move to replenish the glasses. We had been still, watching the dusk for some time. The visit had seen many long periods of silence, but we had been friends long enough to enjoy each other's company without idle talk.

I broke the spell by turning on the light and rummaging through the refrigerator for dinner. Cold ham and potato salad was enough of a supper. It was too hot to eat anything else. As I put the food onto paper plates, Frankie made more coolers. In a few minutes we were sitting, picking at the food with disinterested fingers.

"Well, do you have any ideas on what we can do tonight?"

"Not really. I'd like to go someplace that has all new faces instead of the tired old ones we've been looking at all summer."

Frankie looked away from the table. "I know what you mean. I could use some fresh conversation instead of the same gossip that's been going around."

We finished eating and Frankie picked up the glasses and carried them to the sink. I let my mind run with the dishwater as I contemplated all of New York City. I knew I'd heard of someplace new, just last week . . . Lucy had mentioned it.

"I've got it! How 'bout the place that just opened at Seventh and B? I think it's called Peg's. Well, what do you think?"

Frankie shrugged her shoulders. "I don't know. Is there a huge cover charge? I wonder if they play good dance music? Wonder what the women are like?"

"Well, I heard they have one bar, a D.J., and a couple video screens. If Lucy goes there, it can't be that bad."

"What are we waiting for! Let's hurry and get outta here! What should I wear? I gotta take a shower . . ." Frankie disappeared down the hall to the bathroom still talking. I didn't bother to answer her. What was I going to wear? Did I want to pick anyone up? I decided on a pair of tight black jeans, black high-tops, and new Fruit of the Loom white sleeveless undershirt. "Perfect," I said to the mirror. I looked really good.

Frankie had finished her shower, so I went into the bathroom to wash up. When I came out, she had lit a joint, had the stereo on, and was grinding and gyrating her body to Salt-N-Pepa.

I stood watching until Frankie became aware of my presence in the room. The blood rushed to my head when she asked, "Well, how do I look? Do you think I'll meet anyone tonight?"

"You look great," I growled. "Come on, let's get outta here!"

An hour later we got off the sub and were heading down Avenue B. Frankie was still unsure about her appearance. "You sure I look OK?"

"Don't worry about it. Everybody's going to look at you and ask, who's the hot number?"

"Yeah, you're right. Shit, they ain't seen nothin' hot as us in a long time!" Frankie strutted down the block teasing me.

"Yo! Frankie! This must be the place." "Peg's" glared from a neon sign over the top of a building that once was a gas station. We would have walked by if not for the sign proclaiming it. The outside appearance still looked like a service station, but with the windows painted black. We joined a trio of women who were standing outside. The three were watching the street and looked uncertain about going in.

"Come on," Frankie said. "No point in hanging around out here."

It was dark inside despite the flashing lights on the dance floor. The walls were covered with mirrors, the usual gimmick to make a

Friends

small place look bigger. In this case it only made the ten people look like twenty, and the bartender look twice as bored. There was no place to sit but at the bar, so we settled into a corner anxious to watch women for the evening.

Two hours and six drinks later, the place had filled up. Women that came in together were still standing in the same groups talking among themselves. The single women were sitting alone at the bar or leaning against the wall, depending on whether they wanted to be watched, or were watching. Couples were dancing in their accustomed manner and only the very young singles (who barely looked out of their teens) were dancing with newly acquired friends.

Frankie and I mingled our fill. Weaving through the crowd we said hello to old acquaintances and tried to pick up a few new faces. The bar was too new, the evening still too young, and the crowd too sober for any real partying to be going on. I stopped watching the dancers and turned to Frankie. "I can't stand it. These women are boring. If they aren't boring they're snobs. Let's either dance or go home, I can't take it."

Frankie got up from the bar stool. "Lets dance then. I didn't get dressed to sit all night."

I danced with my eyes closed for the first few minutes getting adjusted to the music, but opened them when I felt someone's hip sliding against my thigh. I looked to find Frankie smiling at me. "You look really hot tonight. I don't know what's wrong with these women."

She danced away from me teasingly. I reached out and gently ran a finger down her back. Frankie turned and asked, "Do you know what you're doing?"

"Who me? I'm not doing anything." My hand brushed her thigh. She responded by slowly licking her lips. I felt a flush spread through my body, and looked away. I finally smiled to myself, made a half-second decision and said, "Let's give them something to look at. They look too bored."

Frankie winked at me. "Alright, they won't forget us here."

She took my hand and we danced for a few minutes just letting our bodies pick up the same rhythm. As she moved away from me, my hand slid across her breasts. She turned, grabbed my hips, and pushed her body into mine. I reached my hand out and tilted her chin up towards my face as she straddled my thigh, looking like we were going to have sex on the dance floor. I was dancing with my eyes closed again, oblivious of everything but the music and the heat from her body inches away. The music changed and we kept dancing, smiling at each other as the crowd started to watch. The sweat was pouring off me. I felt my clothes clinging and enjoyed every moment of being watched with lust by the same women that had ignored us an hour ago. Frankie was enjoying it too. The record changed again, and she growled like a feline in heat. I threw my head back and laughed as we left the dance floor and walked straight out the door, never looking back.

Once outside, we jumped into a waiting cab and started laughing so hard I couldn't tell the driver where to go. We managed somehow to make it home. It was with a sigh of relief that I let us into my apartment. As I closed the door, Frankie leaned me against the wall slowly kissing me on the mouth. The blood started rushing through my veins again. I turned away, embarrassed by the flush of emotion I felt. We were just friends. I never expected or even considered anything else. True, we were best friends, but our taste in lovers didn't match. I told her I couldn't deal with any more that night. I wanted to get some sleep and we'd talk in the morning. This was all so unexpected, I was afraid I'd do something out of rashness that would change our friendship too much.

I pulled my clothes off and reached in the closet for a tee-shirt, keeping my back to her as I pulled it over my head.

This is silly, I thought. We've seen each other undressed many times. I shouldn't be feeling this way. I went into the bathroom to wash up, then climbed the stepladder to the loft bed and found that Frankie had already gotten in, wrapped the sheet around her, and was staring up at the stars out the window over the bed. I got in and lay as close to the edge as possible without falling off. We lay there silently until an airplane crossed over; said goodnight and rolled over, our backs just inches apart.

I got up with the sun, not having slept well. Every time either of us moved we seemed to brush together and every time we brushed together an electric shock ran through me. The shock woke me completely, at least a hundred times. Deciding the best thing to do was take a shower, I took my clothes and marched to the bathroom. The water felt wonderful. I stood and let the spray run down my back while I soaped and resoaped my breasts and stomach. I found myself daydreaming that someone else was seducing me with the bar of soap. Reluctantly I changed the shower to cold water. After my hair dried and teeth were brushed, there was no reason to stay in the bathroom any longer. I decided to see if Frankie was awake.

The door to the loft bed was open and I stood watching the scene on the bed. The sun was coming up golden through the curtain of plants in the window. Frankie was awake. She was kneeling, with her back to me. Her hands were absentmindedly playing with the spider plant. The sheet had dropped off and was lying in a pile on the bed and the sun and plants were silhouetting her nude body in the morning glow.

I crossed the room to the bed.

Brown Mommy

Midgett

While lying on her lap with my nose inhaling the aroma of her pussy, mmmmmmmmmmm it always smells soooo good, I started reminiscing about our relationship. It seems like yesterday that we were both in our twenties stationed at Ft. Mead, Maryland. It was 1958. There she was watching Elvis Presley on the Ed Sullivan Show. I used to watch her a lot when we were stationed in Fort McClullan, Alabama during Basic Training. She was always watching television and I had reservations about disturbing her. She seemed totally engrossed in the shows so I never said a word, just looked, wished and fantasized. I was sad when I received my permanent orders to go North. I didn't think I would ever see her again. Then I found her sitting again, eyes glued to the television.

"Hello," I said. "My name is Jackie," as I approached her during a commercial break. This brown woman was intoxicating, her eyes like black marbles sent shivers through me. I mean "girlfriend" was working my nerves. There she was in the heat of the night. The temperature that evening was ninety degrees. She was sitting in the reclining chair wearing shorts the color of the sun with a matching halter top hugging her full breasts. This female with a burnt toast complexion. She responded to me while her eyes stayed focused on the television screen where Elvis Presley's body was gyrating to the beat of his guitar.

"My name is Delcie," she purred, her name echoing through the sparsely furnished lounge which contained only a 12-inch mahogany black and white television which sat on a rust colored wall-to-wall carpet along with a settee of paisley print wedged in between two end tables with a footstool of the same print. A picture of the Army post hung on the wall.

She took her eyes off the television for a brief moment. "I'm from Boston, and I remember seeing you in basic training."

The rest is history. We were together constantly. It was difficult being a woman's lover in the army during that era. You were always being watched, yet we managed to keep afloat. We befriended two gay brothers who became our constant companions. We took weekend excursions together and vacations when we could maneuver them and although there were witch hunts often, we were able to maintain our relationship for the two-year duration we were stationed at the Army Base.

New York, 1961. Delcie is cuddled up underneath me in a fetus position. Sometimes I feel like a giant to her petite brown frame. My girl is 5'3" tall and weighs a healthy 130 pounds with dark brown medium length hair which she wears in her favorite hair style, a beehive.

I cover her with my massive frame of 170 pounds and standing at 5'9". I was always large even when I was a teenager. I was full grown when I reached 18 and weighed 150. My grandmother used to call me sweetie because she said my complexion reminded her of caramel candy. Unlike Delcie who loves dresses and heels, I usually will wear men's trousers, tailored shirts and loafers. I have curly dark red hair with a few freckles to match. It's cut in a short bob with my hair hanging slightly below my hair line. My job as an accountant in Saks Department store allows me some freedom of dress.

I usually sleep with shorts on. Delcie likes to sleep in the raw. Her back continues to nestle against my flat chest while my fingers start to make circular motions on her navel. For a brief moment she moves her head which is lying on my arm.

I whisper in her ear, "I love you."

She murmurs, "Mmmmmmmm."

I put my palm over her now swollen nipple and make circular motions over her breast.

"Ooooooooooooo, you tease, Jackie."

I continue to massage her breast. I take my leg and wrap it around hers to spread her open for me. My hand now slowly descends toward her stomach, finds her hairy mound and starts to massage the place. I rub the silky forest while briefly touching her clit.

"Please," she moans. My hand moves back up towards her stomach where I massage her slowly and gently.

I then move her over next to me, take off my shorts, look into her dark eyes and say, "This tummy could carry our baby." I continue, "Delcie, would you give me a child?"

"Yes, Jack!! Yes! Yes! Yes!" she says with a gleam in her eyes. She hugs me. "You know, sweetheart, although we haven't discussed the baby issue, when I was talking to my mother, Wednesday, she mentioned to me that while she was talking to your mother a few weeks ago that it would be nice if we had children because they want more grandchildren. I asked her doesn't she have enough? She said yes, but she laughed and said she thinks you would make a great daddy. My mother believes we would make nice parents. Jackie, we are blessed to have our parents and each other."

"I know," I say, planting a kiss on her lips.

Delcie then takes my hand and starts to suck on my fingers. She takes in as much as her mouth will hold, wets my hand down and continues sucking them. She then guides my hand over her breast, stomach, hairs and clit. Now she gets up, lays her body on top of mine with her arms folded loosely around my neck. She kisses me full on the lips over my small mouth. Her arms still hugging me, she whimpers and moans with each kiss as she gyrates her clit on the hairs over my pussy.

"Jackie," she whispers, "I Love you."

Delcie continues to kiss me hard on the lips while I push my pelvis up to meet her clit. She continues to make sounds with each motion. She moves her head into the nape of my neck. I can feel her warm breath as she licks my neck, ears and cheeks. I can feel my cunt getting juicier with each kiss. I take one hand off of Delcie's firm behind and slide it under her pussy. My hand cups her whole pussy. I can feel her clit on my hand moving in a rhythmic motion against the palm of my hand.

"Jackie," she moans, "lick me."

I gently move my arms around her waist and mount her. I kiss her tenderly on the lips, my mouth brushing her slowly back and forth while she sinks her fingers in the curls on my head. My tongue starts the journey of passion.

Slowly my tongue moves down in search of her nipples. It makes circular motions on one as my hand manipulates the other simultaneously. My tongue finds the center in between her breasts and slowly advances to her belly where I lick around the bellybutton. My tongue now finds the hairy muff. I nestle my face in it. She pushes her body up to meet my hungry lips, to satisfy my thirst for her, my aching for her warm juices to fill me. I find her hole, her running well of cum. I push my face into her pussy. It's wet. Her juices drench my eyes, nose, mouth and lips. I continue.

My tongue now finds her love tunnel and maneuvers its way inside her, licking, pushing in and out. I continue licking. Her sounds become louder, "Ahhhhhhh! ohhhhhhhhhhhhhhh!!!!!!!

Although the house is warm on this early summer morning, her body starts to shiver. She says in a low but demanding voice, "Push your tongue in me, put it in me, now, please!!!"

I thrust faster upon demand.

"Jackie!!" she screams. "Jackie!!!"

I quickly mount her again. My swollen clit is very large. Her clit now pushes out from underneath its protector, searching, our bodies trying to connect. I can feel Delcie's nails piercing my back, but I'm numb, passion has overtaken me.

We move in our own rhythm with clits matching, connecting tip to tip. Delcie pushes her clit up to meet mine while I continue to gyrate slowly on her love button. She grabs my ass with both hands and pushes her torso up more into mine to meet my demands. Our clits are now joined together, my juices flowing down in her opening while I continue gyrating my clit on hers. We move, rotating on each other's body, connecting . . . faster . . . faster . . . harder, our bodies now mashing one another's.

We move in a frenzy. Suction noises can be heard from our sweat which is sealing our bodies together. As we move faster liquid overtakes our bodies. Passion, lust and love take charge of our senses. We are entrenched in the sea of love. Delcie comes, I come.

"Jackie, Jackie!!!" she screams. "Jackeeeeeeee," she screeches.

"Rrrrrrrrrrrrrr!!!" I roar in a low base.

We both come again and again.

Spent, I support myself with my elbows embedded on the mattress, arms extended cupping Delcie's cheeks. I mash a kiss on my girlfriend's lips while she hugs me with all her might. We move from passion to calm. Delcie releases her stronghold and I roll over to her side. I lean over, look her in the eyes, rest a hand on Delcie's stomach and plant a brief kiss on her lips.

"Yes, mommy, this tummy will carry our baby."

Baskets and Rugs

Vickie Sears

She was a white lady and right off I knew I didn't have no cause talking to her, what with me being Indian. Getting mixed up with white folks can lead you to lots of problems. And I didn't need me no more problems. Already had me three kids, no man, and a job down to the electric plant what didn't hardly pay pissing money

Weren't no sense making no friend with no white woman. Only thing was that this was about the fifth or sixth time she showed up somewheres where I was. Besides, she'd been in one of my dreams, too. Me and her was walking down this dirt road. The kids was up ahead throwing rocks at nothing, yelling at each other while they was knocking leaves offen trees with sticks. Her and me weren't even talking.

Now I don't know about you, but dreams is real important to me. You have a dream and it tells on you. Even takes you up to your relatives what you never met. Some is dead. Some ain't even born yet, but you know they're your kin talking about things you ought to know. Now I didn't know how come her to be in my dream only she was. And here she was again. Seemed like I was supposed to talk to her.

She held up her hand saying, "Hey." It was soft just like when wind shuffles through cottonwood leaves. I smiled back. Seemed like my tongue had a gauze bandage on it.

I picked a chair in a row up front and looked back on her. She come sat right beside me. It was what I wanted only it weren't comfortable at the same time. Seemed like her shoulders was too close. I tried folding up mine and to slow down my breathing. I kept my eyes stuck right to where the teacher was going to talk, trying to pay the dream lady no mind.

The speaker was another white lady done up all crisp like she just ironed everything the minute before. She was plump and right funny soon as she got talking about women's power and self-assertion. People don't seem to know how Indian women always did have power long time before the white people came. We lost a lot, though, after the men started coming home from places like Germany, Korea and Viet Nam. They was real changed. We got the cars and alcohol and drugs; and then the men, lots of them, just got mean and different. They stopped thinking that taking care of kids was their job, too, like it always was in the old ways. Sometimes even the women got their minds on the bottle more than on the kids. I left my man after Jessie, my youngest, was born. He just got so ugly with his drinking that he weren't even worth a conversation. I thought I could do better on my own, so we packed away from the city and come home to the reservation. The quiet here and the water sounds and the clean air is good for all of us. Things are slower, more normal.

Anyhow, the speaker was interesting. I could see how I didn't do too good at asserting myself. Can't say I ever really thought on knowing what was the things I needed or wanted. I was the oldest of six kids. It seemed normal to be busy taking care of everybody who was below me. Mom and Dad was both gone a lot with the fishing and drinking. I been to some of them alcohol meetings and I guess now I know that the drinking was the most hard thing on the family. I never did want to drink, but two of my sisters and one brother have themselves a rough time. My other two brothers used to have it, only they both been steady in AA for a long time now. Reckon I was lucky.

When the meeting was over, the woman leaned over, asking me, "Want to have some coffee together?"

Almost jumped hearing her talk, but I said, "Yeah."

We got us some coffee out the urn and went over by the door. Walking over there made me feel funny being shorter and browner. Felt like all my friends was watching, only I looked up but didn't nobody even notice. Funny how it is to get feelings all inside your body, but you can't never talk about them or even figure them out half the time.

She said, "My name's Thelma. I've seen you in the village with your kids."

"Yeah. Me too."

Thelma kind of frowned, so I said, "I mean I've seen you around. You was at the last lecture, too. I'm Maiselle. I got me three kids, two girls and a boy. They go from thirteen down to eight years.

Good kids. More smart than I was. They can do all this math what looks like a foreign language to me."

Thelma smiled with a little nod of her head, finishing up her coffee. "Well, I'd better start for home."

Something kinda grabbed my stomach, so I asked, "Wanna walk on down to the water? I was going home that way anyhow."

Thelma looked on me with them green eyes, making me feel warm everywhere, for what felt like three minutes before she answered, "That would be real nice."

It was one of them cold late January days when the sun was soaking into everything, tricking you into thinking there wouldn't be no more winter. There weren't no sound except for the soft smacking of the tide sliding onto the beach. It ain't but a short walk down to the water, but it's a right long beach full up with tide pools with starfish, anemones, muscles, barnacles, and sea animals I don't even know names for. I love being outside on that kinda day when the light has streaks in it that bounce back off the trees and gets brighter the higher up it goes. It just makes it so there ain't no words at all to say how beautiful everything looks in cold sun. I was just feeling it all, having my skin puff up with being so happy when Thelma said, "Look at the light."

She was pointing up into this fir tree where light was spread over the middle of the tree, trying to stretch out to the limb tips bouncing in a nice little breeze what was starting.

I know I looked on her for a long time saying nothing. I shook my head. I was right amazed that she seemed to see it same as me. We walked on down the beach a long ways before we came to a creek with a log over it. She hopped up, sticking out her hand for a steady. I took it, telling her, "Seems like your hand is mighty cold. Might should be we ought go back."

She stayed on the log, looking up to the sky. "Yeah. There's a storm coming. I guess you're right."

When Thelma jumped off the log, I took both her hands up, stuck them together, and rubbed them between mine. I done it with the kids all the time, only when I looked up at Thelma's face, she was grinning. I sudden felt silly and said, "Reckon you ought stick them in your pockets."

She patted my arm, "Would you like some tea? You've never been to my house. I know where you live because I pick up your kids."

I didn't ask nothing because she saw I was puzzled. "I drive the school bus."

"Oh. Kids never talk about the driver, just their friends or if you're late 'cause of snow."

"Yeah, kids are like that."

We walked back to the village and toward a red truck. It was parked in front of the feed store. Thelma said, "I have to get two hay bales. Would you mind?"

I said, "No." She unlocked the truck door, holding it open while I struggled up. There are times like that when it's really embarrassing to be so short. It didn't take long for Frank, the feedstore owner, and Thelma to each pitch a bale into her truck. Then we was off.

Now living on an island is real interesting 'cause you run across everyone, especially all the reservation folks, but there are all these little side roads with water coves hidden behind all the conifers, alder and cedar trees so you can't ever know where everyone lives. Thelma's house was like that — up one of them windey mud roads what slides down in a slick hill ending out on the beach. There wasn't nothing there except this long old log house going gray with the weather. The front porch wrapped from all along the front to each side of the house. There were old redwood chairs lined up facing out to the sound. I was thinking how nice it would be to sit there with some tea, hanging my feet on the rail and looking on rain slice the air.

"I'll put these bales in the corral, then we'll get some tea. Okay?"

I nodded.

"You want to see the horses? They're just out back of the woodshed in the paddock."

I was walking behind Thelma, watching her balance a bale on her thigh and knee with her fingers in a real heft on the wires. She was a right strong woman even with all that sadness living in her eyes. I wondered how come it was she was living in such a big house way out on the far end of the island.

Thelma broke my thoughts. "They're only two bay mares, but they're both really sweet. Molly here," she said, patting the horse on the left with the star nose, "is four and Gladys, there, is six. They both love to run on the beach. Sometimes we go over to Six Point for a real romp. This beach isn't really long enough. It's nice having the time between the morning and evening routes to do what I want. The wetter it is the better old Molly here likes it." She rubbed the horse's noses, slipping each a carrot from her jacket pocket. "Okay, now I'm ready to go up to the house, Maiselle. Is there a special tea you like? I've got lots of flavors. Or would you like coffee?"

"I'd really like some peppermint if you've got it."

The path to the house was concrete flagstones. I told her, "This here's a right fancy walkway."

"Yeah. It's a concession to my liking dry feet and a fairly mud-free house. I inherited it when my parents died in a car accident four years ago. I never thought I'd live here again, but it's been a good decision. I put the stones in myself. It wasn't hard at all. Just heavy. Kept me busy all of the first summer. Got my mind off things."

When Thelma reached the stairs, she kicked the mud off her shoes on the edge of the bottom step. I done it, too. At the top of the stairway she pulled back a screen door what had a rip, pushing open this big door that was half glass. In the glass was a ship sitting in waves. I thought it might could be the most beautiful door I ever seen.

The room we come into was big and full up with heavy old furniture, a braided rug what went clean from the couch all across the room to the fireplace. There was a big stack of logs in an old fashioned wood-box. I was so busy taking in all what I was seeing that I never noticed Thelma had gone off to the right into another room. I suddenly felt shy so I poked my head around the door. The kitchen was as big as my whole living room. There was a wood stove and an electric one, too. The sink was the big double-basin kind deep enough for Saturday night baths. Thelma was looking out to the water while the tea kettle was slurping up water from the tap. One burner glowed a red waiting. There was a wood island going down the middle of the kitchen with an iron circle above it where pots were hanging. All my pots was stuffed into one cupboard.

From the doorway I said, "This is the biggest kitchen I ever seen. Bigger than at the Tribal Center. You must have a passel of kids."

Thelma turned off the faucet and walked over to the stove. Her head was down so's I could hardly hear her. "I live alone. No children. Never had any." She plopped the kettle down then went to the far end of the kitchen where she pulled out some cups with saucers. She stuck them on a wood tray where a glass tea pot was already sitting.

"You want sugar or milk or something?"

"No, thanks."

"Well, I like to have cookies with my tea. Do you like wafers?"

"Can't think if I ever had any."

Thelma pulled out some long thin cookies from a cookie jar bear and put them on a plate. The kettle whistled. She poured water into the tea pot, sloshing it around. She dumped that water out, dropped in some loose tea, then filled the teapot with new hot water. She turned the lid into its slot, then put this little hat on the pot. I reckon I must of looked surprised at seeing such a thing, 'cause Thelma smiled as she picked up the tray. "I like to use the cozy because it keeps the tea hot for such a long time, especially when I'm sitting on the porch. You want to go out there?"

I know I smiled me a big one for getting my wish, only I just said, "Yeah. It'd be real nice to watch the water."

Thelma set the tray on a little table between chairs, then dropped into a chair on the right of the table. She stretched her legs out to the railing. I tried to do it, too, but my legs was too short. We moved up both chairs and the table, then settled in for a chat.

First thing I noticed was the clouds. There was the kind what are fat black ones with white edges all stretched out on the top of the sky. Then there was the ones what hang straight up and down looking like a dirt gray window on a long-time empty building. Them's the ones that move so fast in the wind, coming straight at you with their tails ripping right over the water what is always gray, too, when them clouds come. It was feeling all warm and special like always, so I couldn't say no words on how it was inside of me. I was so caught up with sitting there, seeing them clouds, feeling the cold and the safeness on that big porch, and knowing rain was gonna pelt the roof right soon, I never talked to Thelma at all.

* * * *

Winsome is the only word I could have used to describe Maiselle that day. She was short and chunky, even then, so that her legs barely reached the porch railing although we'd pushed the chair very close to it. Her hair was pulled straight back and clipped with a wide beaded barrette. It made her face look younger than I assumed her to be.

She was all of thirty-six years. There was a shine from her dark eyes that made them hard to distinguish from her hazel-colored skin. I could tell by the way she had concentrated on the clouds that she was seeing past them into their colors and the wind that moved them, or maybe even the water that filled them. She had a curiosity that drew me toward her. I'd seen her so many times I couldn't count them. I'd tried to offer her rides when I'd seen her walking home with both arms full of groceries, but couldn't. I'd tried to talk to her at community meetings and on the ferry dock when we were in line. I always grew too shy. But that day of the assertiveness class seemed like the opportune moment. I never imagined she'd come home with me, but sitting next to her kept my stomach curdling, so I could only concentrate on her not hearing it.

After about ten minutes of silence, I poured some tea through the strainer and passed Maiselle a cup. Now she might remember this differently, but I most decidedly felt a spark when my fingertips touched hers. I knew what it was, but Maiselle looked like it was as much of a surprise as learning what your newborn infant was. Darn near dropped the saucer and cup, but she looked away, saying, "This is the most fancy tea I ever had. We only have mugs to home and just pour in the leaves. Most times the teas we drink are medicine, so you don't want to strain it away from your body."

I said, "I think of the time when I drink tea as medicine because it lets me think and gives me feeling time."

"Yeah. It's like that going down to the creek or the woods or just sitting by the water. It's nicer since the kids don't keep up the racket they used to. Sometimes they get on each other so much, though, it makes you wonder if there's peace anywheres. I even don't know how come it to be that people all over the world ever manage to stay out of wars as much as we do, what with there being so many differences everplace."

We talked like that the rest of the afternoon, not about anything special, but books and life in the city as opposed to the country, her kids, my divorce fifteen years before and hers six years before. Then there were all the things we didn't say or question. We moved into the kitchen a while after the rain had begun and were sitting at the table when Maiselle said, "I don't know where my head's gone, but I got to get on home. The kids will wonder where I am."

I suggested, "Why don't you call now. I'll take you home." I handed her the telephone, going to get our coats.

Once in the truck, Maiselle said, "You'd be welcome to supper if you want. Meatloaf, spuds, green beans and fry bread. Nothing fancy, but I make a mean meatloaf."

I gladly accepted. I couldn't get enough of talking with Maiselle.

After a noisy supper and the quiet of bedtime, we chatted until ten o'clock before I said, "I have to be up at five o'clock to get ready for the bus route. It was nice spending time with you."

As we walked to the door she put out her hand for one of those soft shakes Native women give, but I asked for a hug. There was something of a surprise in it for me. I thought her fat would make her just soft, but that wasn't so at all. She was soft and solid both. She had a firmness that let me know she was full of strength and a certitude about herself. And there was a current that surged into my buttocks, up my spine, fully into my breasts. Neither of us spoke about it as I turned and waved "goodnight" while walking toward my truck.

* * * *

I didn't never have me no feeling like I had the first time Thelma hugged me. I closed the door when I seen she was safe in her truck and kept leaning up against it trying to think what was in that hug. After a time I turned off all the lights, threw some wood into the stove and laid down on the couch. I slipped the quilt we always keep on it over me and lay there looking on the flames grabbing and snapping at the wood. I couldn't get the feelings out from my skin. After awhile I let my hand slip down between my legs and was surprised to feel myself all slick. I said to myself that I was excited because I had me such a good time laughing and talking, only I couldn't get myself to sleep without calming myself down. I started thinking on the clouds moving when Thelma and me was having tea on the porch. My fingers was moving like the clouds in and on myself until there was that jerk that brings the little glow so's sleep can come. But there weren't no easy sleep at all that night. Never have figured out how all the comfort lumps in the couch turned into spring stabs overnight. Every move I made brought Thelma's face flashing into my head. The kids wound up making their own breakfasts while I made lunches and a cup of coffee to take down the path to Thelma. Give her one of the Tlinglt whale mugs a friend brought down from Alaska. Even put some tinfoil over the top so's it would be warm. She stuck her fingers right over mine when she took the cup, giving me a smile.

* * * *

Bringing me coffee was the first time Maiselle ever walked her children down the driveway. I was so touched I couldn't think of anything to say except, "Thank you," but wasn't the brilliance I wanted so it was easier to say nothing.

When I got home from the morning run, my thoughts were crowded with Maiselle. I went upstairs to the front bedroom where I kept my loom. I wanted to make pictures of the day before. Wanted to speak in the way that had always been more potent for me than words how the day had felt. I did a sketch first of the wooded path I drive home on. Then one of the ocean with the clouds falling into it. And finally one of the light on the trees, reflecting in the clouds, because it was the light shifts I knew Maiselle had seen the same as myself. I knew there was a joy in the weave of it so I began. I grew so involved, I almost missed picking up the kids.

* * * *

Thelma brought the cup back the same day I give it to her, only it was full of snow-berries. I grinned and was going to say something when she turned away real sudden and went back to the bus.

I didn't give her no coffee the next day 'cause my mind was just festering thinking about her. I knew it wasn't right to be wondering about how she looked naked or what it would feel like to touch white people skin, yet them thoughts was there. I had to stay away if I wasn't gonna get into trouble. She might even be a waiting to do pony stealing like so many white people do, always trying to learn the stuff what is spiritual. Then they call themselves experts and write books on how it is to be Indian. I'd read some of those books. Also I didn't know why Thelma was living so near the reservation. I made up my mind she was a "wanna be" and felt better right off. For about four days that is. I just couldn't shake her out my mind, but I kept avoiding seeing her.

Come Thursday two weeks later, in the middle of getting supper ready, there was a knock at the door. Laurence, my eldest, answered, but nobody was there. He brought in a long package wrapped in brown paper. We all gathered round to undo the string and roll it open. The note on top the rug said, "To remember a lovely special day. Thelma."

It took all the air out of me to see the sky all full up of draggy gray clouds with light coming out behind them, bouncing off the trees. I had no imagining how come a white person to really see such a thing, even though I felt Thelma had. Right then me and the kids tacked the rug up on the living room wall across from the couch. After supper all I could do was gaze on that picture and wonder how it was Thelma could make the yarn sing so well about the light.

* * * *

Early Saturday, after having delivered the weaving, I heard a car mud-slide into the yard. I pulled on my robe and opened the door. Maiselle was knocking mud off her shoes as I walked toward her.

"Morning. You're up early. It's good to see you," I said. "Want coffee or tea?"

"Coffee, please. I just put the kids on the ferry to visit my sister in Seattle. I wanted to bring you this."

She offered a basket with a lid. Small canoes encircled the basket. A larger one was on the lid. "It's very beautiful, Maiselle. Thank you so much. I'll put it here on the mantle."

She asked me, "How come you to live out here in such a big house?"

I didn't really want to tell her about me just yet. I had fantasies I didn't want to admit to, but it was such a clear request. "This used to be my parents' lodge. There are cabins past the shed on the other side of the woods. My folks ran this place as an inn. I often let artists come stay. My folks left a fair bit of money and investments. I made some myself when I was teaching. I don't have to worry much but I need to work to keep myself going."

Maiselle was quiet, looking through me, listening in a way that I knew would bring the next question.

"Didn't really tell me nothing about you, your answer."

I moved into the kitchen, feeling pain in my hip just from thinking about the accidents. They were major parts of my reason. And the drinking I'd done. I tried to distract Maiselle by asking if she wanted food as well as coffee.

"Toast with jam. Coffee with lots of milk and your answer."

I was quiet until I'd poured coffee, made toast for her and tea for myself. Maiselle had seated herself at the table, sitting perfectly quiet throughout my preparations. I put everything on the table, continuing the silence while Maiselle poured milk into the coffee, stirred the pale liquid into slow circles that took on a life of their own. Putting her spoon on the saucer, she sat back in the chair, folded her arms and looked into my face.

"I guess I'm running and trying to forget. That's all." I said.

"No, ain't all, I reckon."

I smiled. "You push hard."

Maiselle's face furrowed. "Guess so. I'm sorry. Don't mean to pry. You don't got to answer." She put both her hands around her cup, sipping at her coffee.

I touched her right wrist which was closest to me and said, "I think I'd like to tell you, but I don't know you. You might become a friend. Maybe not. I'm just . . . a little scared."

Maiselle nodded.

I poured my tea down my throat, refilling the cup before I spoke. Maiselle continued to enfold her cup and look into her coffee.

"Six years ago my lover died in a rock climbing fall. It was horrible. I started to drink. Couldn't keep up with my job. Even came to work drunk a couple of times. Trickled Scotch into me all day like it was a transfusion. No one said anything for a long time until, one day, I started blubbering at work. The administrator was nice and gave me a leave of absence, but I didn't stop my drinking. The school couldn't wait any longer. I lost my job. I started feeling more sorry for myself. Got to be a regular barfly."

Maiselle nodded, but never said anything. I took a deep breath, trying to finish quickly. "My folks were driving down for a surprise visit, but they hit some fog outside of Big Sur and went off the road. I didn't hear about it for two weeks. The news had to get back to Uncle Charlie, my dad's brother, and then down to me. I only happened to come home after three weeks of being at other people's houses and bars. I was the one hard to find. I went crazy. I got into the car and drove like a mad woman straight into a utility pole. Broke my leg and hip. Spent six months in the hospital, four of them in detox. That was four years ago."

Maiselle put her hand over mine. She didn't speak. I looked down at the texture of her skin, wanting to pull her hand up to my face, wanting to feel her whole body.

I said, "I . . . ah . . . came up here to straighten out family matters. It was so quiet. I forgot how quiet it could be. There was nothing left in L.A., so I stayed. I just kept fighting with the bottle. Then I threw myself into fixing the house and cabins. I started seeing a therapist, trying to not drink. Last year I started driving the school bus. Guess I missed kids. Haven't had a drink in three years now."

Maiselle, still holding the top of my hand, said, "Sounds like mighty hard times what with losing your man and your folks."

There it was. That awkwardness when I knew "lover" had meant "man." I couldn't hold it back. I'd spent too much time doing that. Being a teacher. Being a daughter to parents who never knew. Being a drunk unable to grieve Sharon out loud. So I just said it. "I didn't lose a man, Maiselle. I lost Sharon."

I don't really know what I expected, but it wasn't a cheek kiss.

She said, "That part don't matter. Sounds like things was real hard and you're doing better."

That was that. We talked all day, walking or sitting on the couch and having dinner. During supper Maiselle asked, "How come you ain't asked me how it feels to be an Indian?"

At first I laughed, but looking at her face, I realized she was serious. I asked, "Am I supposed to?"

* * * *

Now it weren't that she was supposed to ask, it's just that sooner or later it seems to come up. Thelma answered me, "Guess I'd rather learn about you as a person, what you think about and how you see things. That makes up how well we get to know each other. Do we want to know each other?"

I remembered that was one of them indirect questions from the assertiveness class, so I asked her, "Does that mean you want to get to know me an' you want to know if I want to be friends?"

Thelma looked down to where our hands was still resting together, so's I couldn't see her face was red. When she come up from her chest, she was grinning, "You got me, didn't you? I never am very straight. Sharon complained about it all the time. Let me try again: Can we explore a friendship?"

"Sounds real formal to me," I said, but you know, there was this toss over in my belly what made me want to leap up with excitement, and made me scared, too. The scared part of me made me take my hand off hers. The excited part said, "Yeah."

* * * *

For almost five months Maiselle and I called each other nearly every day, went for walks, rode the horses, or hung our feet on the porch railing while her kids played on the beach. She started Community College and I finally painted the house. We were going on a picnic one Saturday morning after she had put her kids on the ferry. She arrived about seven o'clock, two hours earlier than planned. I was still sleepy, making holes in the day with my yawns, when I started toward the kitchen to make some coffee. Maiselle put one hand on a shoulder and one in the middle of my back, shooing me into the bathroom with, "I'll make breakfast. You get ready."

Half an hour later I came out showered, dressed, and ravenous. On the coffee table in front of the couch were salsa eggs, muffins, and coffee for both of us. It made me smile to think of her doing such a familiar thing as making a breakfast in my house.

We were quiet through much of the meal when I said, "Is there something on your mind? You seem really quiet."

"Not exactly."

We stayed quiet so long, all I could think of to do was touch her ankle with a pat. I said, "I like your socks." They were white with black zebra stripes. Maiselle had dozens of the most wild socks you can imagine. I was waiting for her birthday to make a trip to the city just for weird socks and a book on astronomy, of which she was a master student.

She looked up, focusing on my eyes, glancing at my hand resting on her ankle, then back to my eyes. I moved my hand up to her calf, gently squeezing. Maiselle never moved. I put my other hand just above her knee on her other leg. I don't remember breathing. I only remember feeling wind come into me through my palms.

* * * *

That morning I never woulda been able to say what was on my mind or how long I'd been waiting on her to touch me the way she was now. In my whole life I never thought on making love with no woman. Especially no white woman. But not all white people are the enemy. Thelma taught me that. She never asked me to tell her "the Way" or take her to a sweat or even show her to dance. She'd listen if I told her things, but she never expected me to give her "the answers." I think I taught her about slowing down. Seemed she was trying to fill all the busted places inside of her with constant doing.

Both her hands was on my legs. I was slick with a wet my man didn't never make, feeling like I couldn't move at all or everything would be gone. I was struck shy, too, so there weren't no words. Only wind knocking feelings inside my body. I touched her cheek like I would one of the kids if they was full up with worry, but I couldn't take my hand away.

Thelma leaned over with a kiss that was soft as newly cleaned deer hide, all soft like baby tummies, only getting firmer as I was letting my own feelings out.

She pulled back, looking on me with question. I didn't know how to say "yes" or "no," only I guess I did, 'cause I took Thelma's hand and was walking to her bedroom. Once we was sitting on her bed I said, "I want you to hug me."

* * * *

That first hug with Maiselle was something I knew I'd been wanting for two years. It was everything to feel her full breasts press against my hardening nipples. I held her a moment before taking a long breath of happiness. As my lungs filled against her, Maiselle made a quick low sound, straightened her body, then dropped her head back over her shoulders.

I kissed her upthrust chin, moving down her throat. She tasted of early-morning air. She unbuttoned her blouse, pulling it back toward her shoulders. I gasped at the sight of raised brown nipples encircled by an areola darker than her hazel skin. I kissed down to her cleavage, beginning a series of short licks there.

Maiselle kept her head over her shoulders, her long hair fluttering against my hands on her back. I circled her left nipple with my tongue, licking over and around it. She brought her hands to my head, pulling me into her breast, while lowering herself onto a pillow. She moaned, pushing her chest against my face as I began to pull on her nipple. I brought up my hand to press against her right breast, my palm making circles.

* * *

After a time of Thelma's touching me, I knew for sure that making love was something there weren't no stopping. I understood that there was aching in me from the first time I'd seen her down to the feed store when she was buying chickens. So I was just gonna do it even if I wasn't for sure how.

I put my hands on her shoulders, rolling her onto her back. Looking straight on her, I started to unbutton her shirt. Thelma raised her arms up over her head. I unbuttoned her shirt, leaving it closed, while undoing her jeans. I took off her shoes and socks before I pulled off both pairs of her pants. I kept looking on her face, scared I would stop if I seen her body like I never seen no woman's body before.

I stood up on the bed concentrating on taking my clothes off. I didn't think it fair for only her to be all undone. I dropped everything over the bedside, then knelt beside Thelma, still not looking on her body, but straight her eyes.

She was crying. I put a hand next to each shoulder, kneeling over her to kiss her eyes. She took in a couple of gaspy tear gulps. I straightened up to spread open her shirt, helping her shrug it off each shoulder. Thelma shivered a little, but left her arms up over her head.

Real slow I took in seeing her whole body. She was like one of her weavings, all done up in beige and pinks with a sun-brown chest mottled with white spots There were moles of different shades of brown, dark red-brown silver-striped hair on her head, fine blonde fuzz over her arms, and a coarse brown-blonde bush, all curled and thick.

She had a purple-blue-magenta bruise right in the middle of her stomach where she fell off the ladder last week, hitting herself on a step corner when she landed. I kissed that place. I touched her bush, working my way up to her hip. I kissed her hip, molding my face into it, running my cheeks over it. I drug my hair over her stomach and slow over her tight breasts. They didn't fall off to the sides like mine. They was small softnesses that was all tight right then.

I come up over her body, putting a leg on either side of her, pulling up high enough to drop my right breast just above her lips. I swung my nipple over her lips and then cupped her face between my breasts. Thelma's hands kneaded them, then started going all up and down my body. She was kneading my butt when she threw one leg over my hip, rolling us to our sides.

Next thing I knew we was touching all over each other. She was the most wonderful thing I ever felt. It was like working with different grasses, porcupine quills and dyes when making a basket. She was the toughness of pounded cedar and the brittle taste of birch as you split it.

The air started filling up with thick sex smells. My tongue was running over her teeth, licking her neck, and then her hand was on my clitoris and the air was all gone in the room. Blood was cutting out every noise except for its own drumming. I lifted my leg over her hip and started rocking. Then her fingers was at my vagina, making circles, and I pushed up to get them inside of me.

Thelma rolled me onto my back, slow moving her fingers in and out, looking into my eyes to somewheres where I never let nobody else ever go. Then the only sounds was the raise of my juices sucking in and out of me as her fingers moved, and me moaning with Thelma touching inside like no man ever done.

It started being more than I could stand with me wanting to do something more than thrash my head side on side. I didn't want it to be over. I put my hand on her wrist and Thelma stopped. I folded her in my arms, going to my side. We was both panting for quite a time before I felt my crotch slow down enough to kiss her real quiet on the mouth. When I came away from her mouth, she was smiling.

I let my hands roam, then leaned over to look at her back. She rolled onto her stomach. I started kiss her back, moving down to her butt. I dragged my hair up and down her back and over her butt. I kissed her thighs, kneeling over her with my butt toward her head. I was studying her feet and squeezing her calves when Thelma starting to hump on the bed.

    I licked the inside of her thighs, stroking my hand in her butt crack, getting hotter with her sounds and moving. I turned Thelma to her side, putting my arm between her legs. She squeezed on it. I started kissing her bush and rubbing that fur all over my mouth. The smell of her was all hot, claiming all my senses.

    Keeping my arm where it was, I turned Thelma more on her back, putting my body down onto her stomach, not caring I would make her all sticky with my rubbing on her belly. I started taking little nips on the inside of her thighs and before I knew it, I was kissing on her vagina and running my tongue clean over her lips and that hard button up to the top. When I done that she jerked, making more noise than I ever remember coming out of me any time I was ever sexual before.

    I wasn't sure she liked it, so I got more soft. Pretty soon she was pumping up and down, and I was holding open her legs on her thighs, loving looking at her and feeling vibrations in her thigh muscles. She arched to let out a wild sound that lasted what was forever in her having spasms for such a long time. She flopped quiet while I lay with my face full into her crotch, feeling her blood humming in my ear.

*　*　*　*

    We made love all day, with Maiselle spending the night. I woke with sun spilling across my face, rich in the smell of unwashed sex. I leaned on my elbow to watch Maiselle sleep.

    Maybe some people don't think seeing into a woman's body is like looking at her spirit, but it has always seemed so to me. I came down on Maiselle's vagina slowly the day before, long into the afternoon, with only puddles of sun daubing her skin. Her acquiescence to letting me look at her was not immediate. I stroked the tops of her thighs a long time until I felt her muscles relax. I asked her if I could part her labia. While she said it was alright, she turned her face sideward. Her lips were a brown-violet covered with glistening juices. I folded them aside, using my index fingers to part her vagina. She was ruby-magenta pink and browns thick with fluid, swollen with desire. Her smell was briny invitation. I took a fingerful of her, rising over her cookie-soft body, partially lying on her. She had turned her face to me. I ran my finger under my nose, pulling her smell inside, before I encircled it with my tongue. Maiselle's eyebrows rose in surprise. She said, "Do that to me."

Moving back down, I opened her lips, holding them, dipping my tongue into her vagina. I put a finger against my tongue to slowly stroke her while sliding my lips over one then the other labia. I began to create circles just inside her vagina with my tongue, slowing and quickening. I pressed against her clitoris, just holding it, barely moving my tongue in an occasional flick. Maiselle began to clutch at my shoulders, clamping and unclamping her fingers, until she stiffened in orgasm. I laid on her body, holding her, feeling her power.

* * * *

That first time was sixteen years ago. Thelma and I have been living together since two years after that time. Things aren't done so quickly now, but making love with her at fifty-one is as rich as ever was any basket or rug. And it doesn't matter about her not being Indian. She's my lover and best friend.

Letter Home

Sabrina Sojourner

Hi Sweetie,

How was your day today? Mine was emotionally excruciating. This project is turning into a real monster—much like some of the jerks I'm having to deal with. Sometimes I don't care how inappropriate it is to wish for a world minus men, especially white men. These feelings arise every time someone lives up (or down) to their stereotype. You guessed it. Michael and I got into it again. But I'll talk about all that when I call.

I miss you. It would be heaven to be home right now in your loving arms. I want to feel them enfolding me like the wings of an eagle. I want to feel your lips against my forehead. I love the soothing, loving energy that blossoms and radiates through my body when you do that. I like to let myself be blanketed in its calmness. It lets me know that I am definitely at home.

Sweet woman, I long to indulge in long, deep kisses. Soul kisses. Have you ever wondered why they're called that? When I think of us soul kissing, I get images of warm breezes, lazy white sand beaches, and the hot sun kissing my honey brown skin. Here is where I travel when we kiss: a safe and beautiful world where our spirits can meet. We are far away from bigotry and hatred as we bask in the warmth of our love and the light of its beauty. In this world there are only people who love and care for one another and themselves. People who know the value of sharing and appreciating goodness. In this world we know that anything this loving, this affirming of self is right and blessed.

Beautiful lover, my sweet friend, I lie here touching myself, pretending that my hands are yours. Knowing that on some level they are, for only you know my body as well as I — if not better. Your touches teach me. Your touches reach me, open my doors and invite me out into the sunny meadow of hope and happiness. I've learned so much about myself through knowing and loving you. I'm learning to be more honest and less afraid. I didn't realize how scared I still was until you started pushing to get past that barrier. I know you did it for yourself and not for me. Whatever the reason, I'm glad it happened. Where once I perceived a desert, a forest of imagination and fantasy is now enjoyed, nurtured by your love and my love of self.

Damn! I wish you were here. If you were, I would invite you aboard the barge of fantasy. We would sail to that place where our love is blessed. We would swim in warm rivers, flowing with the subtle shifts in currents. We would feed on the honey of our love; bathe in its nectar. I love eating you. Scooping your juices out of your cunt like I'm eating ice cream. I like putting my mouth over your cunt and running my tongue over and over your clit until you let loose a moan that lets me know you are with me. I laugh as I write this. It's so "politically incorrect." Your separatist friends (who already don't like me) would probably threaten to kidnap one or both of us if they were to read this letter. Is there another way to describe exchanges of power and letting go when we talk or write about sex?

I mean, I love fucking you and I love it when you fuck me. And saying, "Oh, baby, penetrate me!" when we're thick in heat just doesn't cut it, you know? Yeah, Baby, you know. Baby, why aren't you here? I would love to be inside you and feel your hot, wet pussy surrounding my fingers. The soft unevenness of your sweet, salty flesh. I wish I could find the words to describe the sensations which ripple through me as your pussy contracts around my hand, or my fist when your pussy's real hungry. It's more than just being close. It's an incredible kind of sharing and intimacy I've never experienced before.

I am so wet, I could easily get three of my own fingers inside me, right now! I would love to have three of your fingers inside me. Or your beautiful brown fist. I think I just let loose a wave of pussy juice. I'm sure I'm sitting in a puddle. I just flashed on us making love last night. I love how you suck my breasts. I know I've told you that before. Of course I've also told you how much I love how you kiss me, hold me, tease me. Let's face it, I love having sex with you.

Well, honey, I can't stand it anymore. I'm going to stop and go get myself off. I wonder what I'll fantasize about? Any suggestions?!?

I love you and miss you. See you soon.

One August

Pearl Time'sChild

August 2, 1982

My lover is gone for a few days, giving me a stretch of needed solitude. As it happened, the day Jo left, the book *Coming to Power*[1] came into my hands, s/m stories published by Samois, the lesbian s/m group. Reading it has left me erotically touched. But also with many doubts and complex feelings. I had thought I was pretty much convinced not to be frightened of what is within me. Now I don't know. I am afraid to think about, write about, s/m. I don't know if it's something I should flee from if I value my life, or if it's only another closet in my mind. The parallels to coming out as a lesbian are mockingly clear. And the differences.

At this point there's not a whole lot to come out about in terms of my experience; there is a lot I could confess as to fantasies when I am with myself. I want to say they are not so terrible as all that; and yet on one level they are. I don't feel perfectly all right about having them; I do not look forward to watching it all in detail with the White Light by my side looking sadly and compassionately on. I do not like to think about the amount of time my mind can spend hanging out in those places while I could be out seeing the beauty of the world, the blue sky, the clouds, the seasons, the gifts of color and joy to the eye.

When I think of it in this way, then investigating one's s/m side does seem to me to be a wrong turn. I feel totally vulnerable to the judgement of someone who spends her time working with developmentally disabled kids or any number of other useful pursuits, to his/her judgement that anyone who puts time into investigating this underground self deserves to be squashed underfoot like any cockroach. . . . The size of *this* closet is enormous. In the past few days, since I read those stories, I have felt so alienated, from my daughter, from the women in my worship-circle, from so many other women, and from the homely tasks of carpentry and housekeeping — the whole busy, daylight world, and my own upstanding self in that world. Knowing. The amount of erotic power that comes in opening up to those images. Some of them.

There's so much to say and I'm afraid to say any of it. Papers can be evidence. How do those people who are involved in s/m manage to live their lives that far from the pale? This is blowing my image of myself as not controlled in my own mind by what society thinks. But I'm not sure I could live so far off the track from what the world thinks and stay sane myself. It's hard enough to be a lesbian and sane in a straight world.

I also feel anger at a mass culture that seems to me extremely pornographic in its approach to sex, and brings all the wrath of the hypocrite down on someone who will allow those messages to be heard at a conscious level, who will consider the possibilities of acting out. Still . . .

"We are here in this life to love," says Elizabeth Kübler-Ross. "Nothing else really matters." I believe that. How can I then be at this moment so obsessed with this matter? Should I not flee? Is this just the month for everyone to be crazy?

But *is* this crazy, or is this love itself? Is it love to learn not to oppress those friends of ours who have not been afraid to explore the power, the erotic power, that comes to them in this way.

Safely. Lovingly. Secretly.

Safely? Lovingly? Always?

"I don't like the personality changes I've seen in my friends who've gotten into it," says Carrie, her voice full of hurt. "I liked them better before." They isolate themselves together, she says. She speaks of things done by "people I know, people I've cared about, and respected. I'd rather not *know* that about them." Which may sound like a snippy comment when I write it down, but if you could only hear the sadness in her voice. And this is certainly not a woman I can suspect of simple closed-mindedness or prudishness in sexual matters.

Yet the parallels are obvious: The complaints of straight people that the gays tend to group together. The "why do they have to talk about it?" syndrome.

I, who am still struggling for the courage to say the word "lesbian" to my father, am thinking: What would *that* closet be like? Knowing one could expect no understanding, no quarter, from all but a tiny few.

One August

And as the question once arose as to whether lesbians were a politically tolerable liability for "the women's movement," so the question now arises whether it's fair to ask lesbian rights to include supporting lesbian s/m within its purvey.

And what could possibly be the relative merits of crusading for s/m rights or trying to stop the nuclear arms race?

Still, suddenly I feel like such a hypocrite in some things I've said or written that may have left some friends of mine feeling the way I feel when someone makes a remark about lesbians, friends who may have had experiences that fall within what's called s/m.

. . . Sometimes today a phrase comes to mind from a story Jo wrote recently, as if it were a key: "In love between women, innocence may be entered, and power absolved."[2]

Morning, August 3

Amazing how much sexual power the thought has, the thought of actually opening a bit to those places. It's too much. I'm feeling obsessed, coming more often than in years, feeling tumescent most of the time. But what a pleasure to feel again the power of sexuality!

In the last couple of days I've reread some of the stories and seen them differently. The "Marnie" story (about a spanking), and the orgy story, and one essay by a woman on her own experience, which spoke of the spiritual side-by-side with the s/m-sexual.[3] (My that word was hard to write.)

I am full of thoughts this morning. Wondering about s/m and the old religions . . . Imagining . . . when sexuality was a tool for spiritual teaching, when the use of the power and pull of sexuality was an art tuned to producing leaps of spiritual understanding. Then were lessons taught about surrender? And how pain can be transformed?

And later when they died, did they find Her waiting with the tenderest of kisses for all their spirit withstanding that ultimate humiliation, death? Was this dying much like a road they had traveled once before? When kind sisters took them to the place beyond the ego. [The Goddess, after you die, revealing herself as the Ultimate Compassionate Top. And your pain consensual after all.]

Were those people in their living more able to deal with fear? With pain? With humiliation? With anger? To have these emotions harnessed with the positive power of sexual energy, and to be taken to a place where opposites are reconciled could be a form of spiritual healing, a profound sort of teaching.

In the orgy story, a woman is put into a swing of some sort and whipped. (Another hard word to write in my journal.) The intensity of the situation propels her into an alpha state—total calm, and awareness only of the present, a state where linear thought is almost beyond reach.

Anyway, about the swing — I don't know what it's like, exactly, but it made me think of witches' cradles. All I know about *these* is that after LSD was made illegal, in order to continue consciousness research, some investigators used a device called ASCID. It was a swing of a special sort into which the subject was put, blindfolded; the experience was evidently sufficiently disorienting to simulate taking acid. And *it* was patterned after an ancient device called the "witches' cradle."

All right, all right, but why not take acid and stick to vanilla sex?

Were people more able to deal with fear and pain? They certainly had more fear and pain to deal *with*.

"We are never given more pain than we can bear," says Lavinnia in my worship circle. "No," says Rosanna, "and it seems like we're never given *less*, either." If there's possibly something to this, *is* it a good idea to increase one's capacity to bear pain?

. . . Pain. Pain and the edge between pain and pleasure. My nipples have been sore these past few days. It reminds me of when they were growing, a soreness I found pleasant. It reminds me of when I was nursing, a feeling that meant I was feeding a new life from my breasts. It reminds me of why they are sore now, reminds me of sexual power and surrender, many times a day. It reminds me, above all, of my nipples themselves, tips of vulnerability on my soft womanness.

This soreness makes me think of when my teeth were being straightened. Other kids complained of pain on the days after their braces were tightened, as teeth were pulled into new places. To me, it didn't hurt enough to be called "pain"; there was a pulling sensation, a hurt that was satisfying. LIke stretching one's muscles in ballet.

But is it really all right that my nipples are a little sore still, several days after the fact? To warm a fanny with a hairbrush may do no harm at all, even good, but where does it end? S/m could be dangerous for the body. (So can mountain climbing.) A great deal of attention is paid to safety, of course. (As in mountain climbing.)

* * * *

August 4

Full moon, early morning. Blessed cloudiness. Birds squirting sounds, celebrating moisture in the air, a teasing reminder of spring, or fall. After a night spent mostly wakeful, swimming in moonlight. My womb aching as my ovaries and tubes process yet another egg, complaining more each year at the out-datedness of this ritual. . . . A small pain, but one that made me need the room of sleeping alone.

Sleeping alone.

"It was intense," Jo said, on her return from her trip to visit her new friend. "We became lovers."

"Well," I said, "I must have spent the weekend thinking about fear and pain and how they can be transformed for *some* reason."

I'd known it would come sometime. Needing more solitude, I had been the one to insist on freedom as the basis for our relationship. But now it was she who was making us non-monogamous in fact as well as in theory.

"I'm frightened," I told her. "I *am* frightened. But it's not really that I fear what will happen in the long run, whatever happens. I'm just scared of the next few hours."

It did hurt. It did scare me. It did put me through grief. It did make me want to pull away, to turn to myself. It gave me all those feelings you have when someone is lovers with someone else, that reflex keeping intimate attraction well out of view, knowing if she's lovers with someone else she cannot be lovers with you. . . . I could not imagine that we would ever make love again, that she would ever want me. I could not put my arms around her. It was hard to breathe. When she reached to me, I couldn't let myself feel her touching without a flood of tears. So I just let the pain be, let the tears come. And tried to remember if there *was* something I had learned about transforming pain and humiliation by experiencing them while being held by love.

She was very tired, having hardly slept for days. And frightened, herself, she said, that I would pull away. We went to bed. We talked. We kissed tentatively. I told her about my weekend; and it felt very strange to feel that she couldn't talk to me about hers. When I said that, she offered to talk about it—not knowing what would be best, not knowing if it would hurt.

"I want to try." I told her. "Listen. Stop if I hum 'Jingle Bells.' But if I just cry 'Stop!' Oh, no! Stop!' Pay no attention. It's just me letting it all be."

So she told me about her weekend; busy-sounding, told at that level. But helping to demystify it all. Replacing a blank, filled with projections, with a real woman in a busy, accomplished life full of connected relationships. Jo said that the first night they had fallen into bed and into each other's arms, and that it had been "so easy." There were large blanks of time in the following days she sketched in.

"Have you told me what was intense about the weekend?" I asked.

"Well, we made love a lot."

"Are you in love with her?" I asked. She thought a while. "I feel like I love her." And that changed the fear in my question, for of course I know that there is no contradiction in loving two women. Later she said, "I think you're both terrific women."

It really is all right. And last night as we talked, sometimes there would touch me the delightful feeling of my own freedom, sprouting like a little pair of feathered wings. This woman will help me love her; Jo and I are out from under being a couple. I think this will shatter some patterns that are not good for us. And I am free to seek myself.

It certainly puts Jo in a different perspective, leaving me free to value our relationship without fearing it will swallow me whole. I have been wishing forever that she had an independent life that pulled her and fed her as my own does me.

We talked about whether we should make love. It seemed a good thing to do, to bring the circle whole. Tonight it *would* help to heal and reassure; but we could also wait to reconnect erotically another time. She was tired, and so I held her as she fell asleep, feeling a little like her mother, feeling a little as if she were my daughter venturing out into the world. . . . But when she was asleep I wanted to be alone, to ease my aching womb, to return to the solitude who is my lover, to the sky, and this house.

I spent a wakeful night watching the moon and clouds, and am now awake again early. It was hard to breathe when I woke up; my diaphragm seemed paralyzed by fear. Fear of being left alone to proceed on down the Road To Hell without any touching. Carrie in my dream accusing me of "deliberately choosing a life of loneliness."

One August

Tuesday noon, August 5

I keep returning to the idea of God as Compassionate Top, and your pain consensual after all, and Her kisses on your tears for undertaking to be that naked, for bravely becoming that unique alloy of pain and joy that was the life you chose to live this time.

. . . Jo likes to pick my blackheads. Though at first it embarrassed me to let my lover concentrate on those unpleasant points in my skin, I was also grateful. There were some I was never able to reach. And it *is* luxuriously pleasant to lie in her lap and be groomed. She shows me the big ones, and tells me which ones were hard and which "like mashed potatoes." I am not at all embarrassed any more; these are neutral facts, as they are for me when I am alone.

I can tolerate a large amount of digging. Over the years I have come to associate the sensation with taking care of my skin, with ridding it of little irritations — a satisfying sensation, not a pain to be avoided. But there are some that go too deep on a sensitive spot, hurt too much, and we usually skip those.

After Jo and I had made love yesterday, relaxing, our faces close, perhaps as a final ritual of reaffirmation, she, as is her way, began to look appraisingly down her nose, as if she were wearing imaginary bifocals, and then began to clean things up along my jawline. She proceeded to my chest, and there she hit a painful one. Shameless with trust by now, I thought I'd try experiencing the pain another way. Joking about it, I closed my eyes, experienced the touch as an erotic one, let my breathing come sharp. I was disappointed when it yielded so soon. "These are just little quickies," she said. But there were more. Little sharp bites of sensation here and there on my shoulders and neck, tapping the power in my loins.

---

1. *Coming to Power, Writings and Graphics on Lesbian S/M*, edited by Samois, a lesbian/feminist S/M organization. Boston: Alyson Publications, Inc. 1982.
2. Jo's story was not about s/m; she meant something different by those words.
3. "Marnie" by Dennise Brown, "Proper Orgy Behavior" by J., and "If I Ask You to Tie Me Up, Will You Still Want to Love Me?" by Juicy Lucy. In *Coming to Power*, op. cit.

Texas Two-Step

Ayofemi Folayan

I'm surprised to see YOU here at the dance," Sharon had said, the caustic acid of her sarcasm seeming to corrode her mouth as the words escaped. Her eyebrows arched as she looked pointedly at the aluminum crutches that I now use all the time. I could feel their metallic cuffs pressing into my forearms as I gripped the handlebars for more support. The thermostat in my body ricocheted upward as anger suffused throughout my body.

"Why shouldn't I be here?" I snapped. Tension hummed in the air between us like a high-power line. It was the first time I had seen her since our decision to end our relationship.

"Well, you can't dance any more." Her voice went up about two octaves on the word "can't." She turned back to her new lover, Harmony, grasped her arm, and strolled back toward the dance floor. In my imagination, I hurled a fireball in their direction and chuckled at the image of their scorched butts.

The moment of laughter came and went. All my energy for being at the dance had drained out of me into an emotional puddle that seemed to stain the polished woodwork under my feet. I set the sweating bottle of mineral water into a large plastic trash barrel marked for recycling and went back to my car. As always, when my anger erupts, I drove a little too fast on the freeway coming home.

The anger fueled another nearly forgotten emotion inside me. I couldn't even remember the last time those feelings had lubricated my genitals and caused such a smoldering sensation to ignite my clitoris. Well, maybe I couldn't walk as good as I used to or do fancy dances, but my body still worked in other ways.

I could feel the swollen flesh of my clitoris pressing against the smooth black silk pants I had put on for the dance. I had felt so elegant as I left the house, my gold and black shirt shimmering under the street lights. My anger at Sharon rekindled. Damn her! She had always solved our arguments with sex. One minute I would be furious with her and the next I would start to feel wet. I guess there was something that happened on my face, because she always knew the exact moment when I was vulnerable enough for her to touch me.

I pulled the car into the driveway and turned off the ignition. I fell into the rituals of being at home: I looked around the car to make sure there was no one lurking there before I got out, locked the door, and went inside. I was irritated with the two deadbolt locks on the door to my apartment. Sharon had installed them when she moved in, arguing that she wouldn't feel safe with anything less. Once inside I locked the top lock. I got a minor sense of vindictiveness when I decided on impulse not to lock the bottom one.

I switched on the lights in my living room and sighed. The magical cleaning genie had not appeared in my absence, so the stacks of papers and books that cluttered the couch and coffee table were still in the same arrangement as when I left. Time enough to deal with the mess in the morning.

I went into my room and popped the Mariah Carey tape into my cassette deck. Her sultry rendition of "Vision of Love" oozed into the room, warming it up immediately. I took off my shirt and pants and hung them up carefully. Humming along with the tape, I lit a candle. Its golden glow seemed to brush across my furrowed forehead and I exhaled deeply as my shoulders dropped.

I stretched out across my bed, laying on my back. I let the music float over me as I rolled my neck around to try to unknot some of the tension tied up there. I closed my eyes and sighed again. I could feel the flesh of my clitoris, still swollen from the earlier flush. I reached under my pillow and pulled my vibrator from its niche. The music was just loud enough so that it covered the annoying buzz of the vibrator's tiny motor.

Moving the head of the vibrator in small circles against my labia, I felt the familiar urge to curl my toes that always signals that my body is ready to respond. I rolled my head back even farther, as my breath quickened. Low moans escaped from the recesses of my throat. I willed my body to relax and receive the electronic stimulation the vibrator offered.

"I'm surprised to see YOU here at the dance," the memory of Sharon's high-pitched voice intruded into my thoughts. A shudder rippled involuntarily through my body. I opened my eyes and was back in my bedroom. Mariah Carey's voice continued to keep me company. The candle light danced on the ceiling above me. Sharon was gone from my life. If only I'd had sense enough not to go to the stupid dance, she wouldn't have had a chance to attack me again.

The tape switched smoothly to the second side. I marveled at the technology that saved me from having to leap up to flip a cassette over. I switched off the vibrator, disappointed that I had allowed Sharon to interfere in my life once more. And her new lover! What kind of name was Harmony? I wondered if she were a former flower child who had taken that name in the sixties when everyone was named Sunflower or Waterfall.

My breath exploded from my body in a sigh filled with frustration. Once again anger had scorched away the good feelings and left a bitter emptiness. I closed my eyes and let the voice of Mariah Carey caress my wounded ego.

"I'm surprised to see YOU here at the dance," Sharon's high-pitched voice intruded again into my thoughts. In my mind I resisted the impulse to smash her in the head with one of my aluminum canes and instead hissed, "I'm surprised they let you out of your cage. It must have needed cleaning!" Then I stormed away, clump-clumping the rubber tips of my crutches on the polished dance floor. Behind me, the rapid-fire drumbeat of Madonna's "Vogue" paced the cluster of women dancing.

I kept going, past the sour smell of beer at the refreshment stand, past the pastel streamers of crepe paper, to the parking lot, still fragrant with the smell of oily exhaust from a battered brown Camaro that had just discharged a woman.

She was wearing a huge suede cowboy hat and matching suede boots. Skin-tight black suede pants slithered up her long thin legs to her waist where a bright turquoise shirt was delicately tucked in. Large patterned silver discs hung from her ears and a shimmering silver scarf flowed from her throat. Her bosom rose and settled as she breathed, and a gentle scent of gardenias seemed to waft past my nose. "I'm ready to do some serious shit-kicking tonight!" she exclaimed to no one in particular as her friend roared away. A thick grey haze of smoke filled the spot where the car had been.

Almost incidentally she noticed me and asked, "Many people inside?"

"It's too early. I'd say there are about fifty people trying to have a good time while there's still room on the floor to dance."

"Well, I guess Maxie and I will get a chance to do some Texas-Two-Stepping tonight." She laughed and I was charmed by the deep warbling quality of her voice. She extended her hand, with long rough fingers, and apologized. "I guess I forgot my manners. My name is Mercury MacClellan. And you?"

"Karen Xavier." As she gripped my hand, a surge of heat suffused my skin. My hand seemed almost to glow from it.

Maxie walked up at that moment to rejoin Mercury. "I had to park back in the state of Texas," she complained. "It must be jampacked in there."

"According to Karen, there aren't many folks in there at all," Mercury reported, nodding in my direction.

Maxie acknowledged me with a nod and the brief introduction, "My name's Benita Maxwell, but almost everyone calls me Maxie." She clipped her car keys onto the belt loop of her faded denim jeans and then shoved both hands into her pockets. "Well, I sure wonder where all the cars came from." As if to answer her question, a side door of the Community Center opened and the sounds of forties Big Band music escaped as an older gentleman in a white suit and straw hat emerged.

"Great," Maxie said. "We have to share the facilities with the Geritol Gang."

Mercury tugged on Maxie's arm. "Let's go inside and get some frequent flyer miles. You won't even notice that other group." She smiled in my direction. "We'll see you inside."

I pulled the brim of my black hat down to the upper edge of my eyebrows and went over to one of the cement benches that bookended the doorway. Mercury had managed to make me forget the remarks that had sent me scurrying outside in the first place. My nose tickled at the memory of her perfume. Curious to see more of her, I went back inside.

Sure enough, in the middle of the floor, she and Maxie were dancing. I spotted an empty seat at the end of the room farthest from the refreshments and made my way to it. Sliding my crutches inconspicuously beneath the metallic folding chair, I watched them until there was a break in the music. Mercury looked around and spotted me. She waved, then stopped for a moment to whisper something to Maxie before coming toward me. Maxie extracted a single cigarette from the pack in her shirt pocket and headed outside.

Mercury beamed in my direction as she sat on the empty chair next to mine. "Is your dance card all full, or will you save one for me?"

Bitterly, I muttered, "Take your choice." The velvet voice of Anita Baker came through the loudspeakers, singing "Fairy Tales."

"How about this one?" Without warning, she pushed her chair even closer and took my arm. She laid her head against my shoulder and swayed with the rhythm of the music. "Karen, where have you been all my life?" she whispered into my ear.

"Are you always such an outrageous flirt?" I countered.

"Only with the women who matter."

"What about Maxie?" I looked nervously toward the door to be sure that she was still on her cigarette break.

"Maxie is my best friend, but we decided a long time ago it was smarter not to be lovers," Mercury answered. So that explained the subtle distance I had already detected between them. "We bought a duplex together about three years ago. Max stays upstairs with her two dogs, and I live downstairs with Maxwell Smart, my parrot."

"Does your parrot talk?" I was trying to continue making normal conversation, but for some reason, my pulse kept racing ahead of my thoughts. Breathing deeply, I tried to calm myself down before the appearance of the inevitable spring of perspiration that flowed when I was nervous. In my head, I began to give myself a pep talk. Keep calm. There's no reason to get nervous. You're just sitting here at the dance holding a beautiful woman in your arms. The music ended and Mercury sighed.

"I don't really want to talk about my parrot right now, Karen, if it's all the same to you." She held onto my hand and squeezed my fingers. "I never know what to talk about when I first meet someone, so I guess I could talk about the bird, but I want to make a good impression on you, and it feels like I'm sounding really stupid."

"No, that's my line," I interrupted. "I am surprised that we are sitting here talking at all. I've gotten used to people just sort of walking past me as if I'm not even there."

"Tell me what turns you on."

"Besides you?" I grinned and continued. "My writing is the most important thing in the world to me. I could wake up in the morning and write all day if I didn't have to work for a living."

"That sounds fascinating," she said.

"It's like having a whole group of friends who are always ready to hang out and tell you about their lives. I'm never bored. These characters just come and take over sometimes." I was aware of the softness of her hair brushing against my neck. It made my breath catch in my throat as I tried to keep my breathing even.

Maxie shifted so that she could look at me. "I wish I had something that I felt so intensely about. I just get up and go to work every day. I come home and the most exciting thing in my life is fixing the food for my parrot's dinner."

"For a long time I was the same way, except that I didn't have a parrot." Vaguely I was aware that the room beyond our little circle of conversation had filled with other women and the lights had gotten dimmer. I could see Mercury's lips and felt a powerful impulse to kiss them.

"Go ahead, nobody's watching," she suggested.

"You don't know what I was thinking," I temporized.

"Wanna bet?" she teased.

The pounding bass of the new Whitney Houston song, "I'm Your Baby Tonight," insinuated itself into my brain, driving the subtle fever inside me. If we were in a movie, the camera would pull slowly into a closeup of the two of us as we fused into a passionate kiss. Fortunately, I had the good sense to turn the vibrator back on somewhere in the middle of this fantasy. As the image of Mercury faded, the gentle hum of the vibrator merged with the music coming from the cassette tape deck. I strained to hold on to the images of the illusion, but they continued to fade.

I could feel my body moving toward a climax. I reminded myself to keep breathing and uncurl my toes, tricks I had long ago learned would help me to stay relaxed and physically present. My body did its usual convincing imitation of a person having a seizure as it reached orgasm, thrashing and jerking with the intense ripples of feeling that pulsed outward from my vagina to the roots of my hair. The tape switched back to side one and Mariah Carey sang "Vision of Love" one more time.

Confessions of a Lesbian Groupie

Carolyn Gage

I went backstage immediately after her number. I couldn't wait for the rest of the show. Who wants to see a bunch of drag queens anyway? But this woman . . . well . . . she had been something else. When a woman wears male drag it's an entirely different thing. It's not an impersonation of a man. Why would any lesbian want to do that? It's a celebration of a third species, as Wittig calls us.

And I mean, she was another form of life. She wore ripped jeans, which looked like they'd been painted on. And she sang this song, "I Want Your Sex," like no man could ever sing to women. I mean, when a man says that to a woman, you know what he means. If he's old-fashioned, it means he wants to stick it in. If he's up on all the latest discoveries about women's bodies, it means he wants to show off what he's learned. But when this woman looked at me and sang, "I want your sex," I knew what she meant and it had to do with celebrating me, and it didn't have anything to do with that other shit.

And that's why I got up and went backstage so quick. I didn't want to let the moment pass.

I had to wade through a lineup of drag queens backstage. This was a lesbian/gay prom night, and most of the entertainers were the queens. In fact, Rusty was the only woman who had the nerve to appear in male drag and do a number.

I found her dressing room. She was in it, flushed with excitement and covered with sweat. She looked pleased to see me. I told her that I loved her act. She kept being flushed and distracted, and thanking me. She was taking off her makeup. I don't think she was getting the message.

I kicked the door closed, and stood up. I decided to take a blunt approach. "Look, Rusty, did you mean what you said when you said, 'I want your sex,' because I sure as hell want yours."

She stopped what she was doing. Maybe that was a little too blunt, I thought. Now, I'm embarrassed. She's considering the offer. Fortunately, she didn't have to think long. I mean, I'm older than she is, but not bad looking. In fact, there're days when I could just fuck myself, and I usually do. There're other days when I think I'm kind of too skinny, or a little too intense, but that's only when it's rained all day.

"You wanna go somewhere?" she asks me.

"Yeah."

"I've got my truck."

"I just live a few blocks from here."

"Okay, let's do that."

"Can you leave now?"

"Well, I'm on again in an hour and a half, if that's enough time for you."

"Sure." I smile. I'll probably come when she takes my clothes off. Or when I take hers off.

Well, I won't bore you with the details. We go to my studio apartment. I don't have a real bed, so I fold down the foam sofa. I mean, an hour and a half and we've already lost fifteen minutes of it. Not a time to be coy.

"After you." I gesture to the foam. Rusty ignores the gesture. Instead she moves close to me and positions one of her legs between mine. Not aggressively. Just efficiently. And then she unbuttons the one button on my jacket and slides it off my shoulders. I realize the light's still on. I reach out a hand to turn it off.

"Don't. I like to see," she says.

"Believe it or not," I tell her, "I'm shy."

She laughs. I turn out the light. She's pressing her thigh into my clit. It reminds me of when I was a little girl and I would straddle the arms of the sofa to play horsey, and ride back and forth on my magic spot. Rusty's hands are gently stroking the skin on my upper arms, almost thoughtfully. I appreciate that she doesn't just go for my breasts right off.

And then very slowly she leans in and kisses me. Her hands are touching my upper arms so lightly I can barely feel them. But she's holding me just the same. And she kisses as slow and as light as she touches. I think my heart's going to stop. I feel her lips on my neck.

Catching my breath, I reach my hands around her waist, touching her as gently as she touches me. I feel the folds of her tee shirt above the jeans. I caress the fabric so lightly, I'm not even touching her body, but I can feel her respond. Her thigh is telegraphing to my clit. And we stand like that for a minute. And then she begins to take off my shirt. It comes off over my head, so she pushes it gently up over my breasts, careful not to touch them. I raise my arms and she pulls it off over my head.

Now I feel very vulnerable. I'm glad it's dark. She reaches a hand towards my breast. I catch it. "Take yours off, too." She hesitates for just a second, and then strips off her tee shirt. She waits for me to touch her. I appreciate that. She must understand some things. Maybe they were done to her, too.

I take my hand and center the palm over her nipple. Then very slowly I press it towards her breast until my hand is cradling her tender breast, as if it were a baby bird. I can feel her moan. She lets me stroke her breast, until I lower my face to lick her breast, to pull on the nipple with my lips, to brush my cheek against her lovely skin.

As I bend to her, she spreads her fingers across my back, gently feeling and holding at the same time. I kiss my way softly to her mouth. We kiss a little deeper now. And she touches my breasts while we kiss.

"Let's lie down," she says pulling back from me, but taking my hands.

I don't say anything. I can't. We sink to the bed. Rusty lies to the side and looks at me. It's dark, but I can feel her looking at me, and I like it. The bed is always a hard part for me.

"We can just do this if you want to," she says. "I'm happy."

I take her hand and hold it to my face. I'm happy too.

With her other hand, she reaches over to stroke my arm. She talks about the sky. It's a clear night, and the stars are out. I move very close to her. I feel her turn towards me. I can feel her breasts against my arm.

"Would you like to kiss again?" she asks. I'm smiling in the dark. I turn and kiss her. She keeps it very slow. I'm the one who pushes for more. I move my face over her. She's lying back looking at me now. I look at her, too, for a long time. And then we kiss again.

"May I kiss your breasts?" she asks. I move over her so that her mouth can reach them. Rusty's tongue is like some tender brush, painting love on my nipples. I feel her passion, but I feel her restraining it. Because she knows I'm scared. Because there's nothing more important than being there for your partner. I like this woman. I'm impressed. I take her hands while she sucks my breasts. I pull her hands over her head and then I kiss her again. I kiss her with all the passion I can see she's trying to control. She lets me set the pace for us.

I sit back and put my hands on her jeans. She settles her hips and folds her arms behind her head. I smile again and unbutton her jeans. She lifts her hips so I can slide her clothes down. Her pubic hair is red. It's a quality you can almost see in the dark. When I get her jeans down to the middle of her thigh I stop and look at her. And then lightly, I brush my fingers through her pubic hair. Getting acquainted. I smile at her. She's watching me.

My finger finds her clit and I trace around it so lightly she has to press her hips up to meet my finger. I bend over and kiss her hair lightly. I nuzzle my nose up against her clit, and I hear her take a breath, her body tense. She tries to open her legs for me, but she can't because her pants are still around her thighs. I press my tongue between her thighs, and I taste how wet and salty she is. I feel her hands touching my head. She runs her fingers through my hair as she raises her pubis to my tongue.

Suddenly she is sitting up. She says, "I have to take my clothes off. I want you to really eat me." I'm flattered. She strips off her pants and wraps her legs around my body. We hold each other in a tight embrace. "Take off your pants," she whispers. "Or let me take them off."

"You can undo them, but I want to take them off," I tell her. She says all the right things.

Rusty rolls me gently over. She looks at me again. We smile. She moves her hand over my clit. I can feel the warmth of her hand even through the denim. And then suddenly she slides herself down between my legs. She is licking me and nudging me through my jeans. I laugh. "Oh, did I forget something?" she asks. I like this woman. I really like this woman.

With her cheek lying against my hip, to the side of the zipper, she opens the top snap and begins to pull the zipper down so slowly it moves over one set of metal teeth at a time. She acts like this is the most exciting part of the evening, like we have all night. I'm self-conscious. I laugh and I reach down to unzip them myself. She brushes my hand away and continues to undo the pants one millimeter at a time. I give up and lie back, smiling at the ceiling. This woman is taking me somewhere I don't even understand, but I want to go. Oh, do I want to go.

Finally the zipper reaches the bottom. "You got any more zippers anywhere?"

"No. That's it." I sit up and she rolls to my side again. I take off my pants quickly, self-consciously. I sit self-consciously, cross-legged. Rusty rolls away from me. She hooks her arms behind her head again, letting me know they're not going anywhere in my direction. She starts to talk about constellations. She wants to rename them. It doesn't help. I'm sitting cross-legged. Scared.

"You know, this is just fine," Rusty says. I start to cry. Fortunately she can't see that's what I'm doing. "You're here and I'm here and we're lying here and we can see the stars, and I can't think of anything I'd like to do more."

"I thought you wanted me to eat you," I say, trying to sound funny about it.

"That was before I got to play with your zipper. Now, my life is complete. I've known perfect bliss."

"You're a liar."

"Well, actually, you're right. I'd like to hold your hand. I know we just met, but could I?"

I laugh and I give her my hand. I appreciate what she's doing.

She holds it just for a minute. Then she holds it against her face, the way I held hers earlier. And I can feel her pressing her lips against it. I get scared, and at that very second she stops.

"Carolyn, if you want to talk about anything, I'm here, you know."

"No. There's nothing to talk about. I just get scared."

"So do I."

"Guess we ought to go find other people who aren't then."

"No," she says. "No." And she takes my hand up to her face again and holds it very still. I can feel her breath on the back of my hand. I feel frozen in time.

"Guess you need to be getting back to do the second set."

"Not yet."

"I don't think I can do anything else."

"That was plenty for me."

"Oh, sure."

There's nothing more to say. I feel miserable. And older and skinny, and it hasn't even rained all day. In a minute she's going to get up and put her clothes back on, and I'll look somewhere else while she does, and then we'll say some stupid things and then she'll leave, and then as soon as she gets out the door, she's going to shake her head and start thinking of how she's going to describe me so that people will laugh when she tells this story about her big groupie.

She lets go of my hand. I look away. I can hear her putting her pants on. I wish I knew what I was doing, or who I was. At least I don't fake it anymore.

She hands me my shirt. I reach out for it, not looking at her.

"Wait." She takes it back. "Let me dress you."

"That's stupid. It's easier for me."

"No, I mean it. I want to."

I'm still looking away from her. I shrug. She takes my hand and threads it through one sleeve, and then she repeats it with the other. She's so careful and so serious about this, I start to smile. And then she lifts my arms and pulls the shirt down over my head.

"May I put your pants back on, too?" I turn my face away again, but I'm smiling. This woman is really something else.

She's taken the underwear out of the mashed up jeans. She threads my feet through as if they were made out of something that would break. And then she begins to slide my underwear up my legs. She has a look of concentration like she was figuring out the wiring on the back of a stereo or something. I start to laugh. She adjusts them over my hips.

"You know, you're really beautiful." She says it offhand, the way she made the remark about renaming the constellations.

I don't have to say anything, because she's already back at the end of the bed straightening out my jeans.

"Those are going to be harder," I tell her.

"Not harder," she says. "Just slower." She pauses for a second. "There's a big difference." She throws that one away, too, so I don't have to react to it. I don't know what to say. This woman is walking me through my nightmares.

She's right. The jeans are slower. But not harder. I begin to relax. She gets them up over my thighs.

"Would you mind if I kissed your clit good night before I tuck her in?" I laugh. She's so serious. "It's okay?"

"Yeah. I guess."

Rusty bends over me. She traces some light patterns with her nose on my thighs. And then she opens her mouth wide and moves it close up against my whole vulva, underwear and all, and she starts breathing out gently into the fabric. I feel a rush of warm air spreading all over my genitals. It just keeps getting warmer and warmer. I laugh. And then she kisses me on the clit, real quick, the way a kid would kiss her great aunt's cheek, if her mother told her she had to. And then she pulls my jeans up. And she zips them up and snaps them together.

"A job well done," I say.

"Anytime," she says.

"You mean that?" I ask.

"Yeah, I mean that. I'll even take them off if you want me to. But putting them on is really my thing. Not too many people specialize in that."

"Rusty, thank you."

"Thank you."

I put my arms around her. She holds me tight, but with all that gentleness. I don't know how she does that, but it's perfect. I tell her.

She takes my face in her hands and kisses me again. It's very different from the kiss a half hour ago. It's light years different. It's the kind of kiss when you've been on a dangerous mission together, and you didn't know if you'd both make it back again, but here you are, and you did make it together, and you're both so glad.

She stands up and pulls me up with her. "Let's go." She's holding my hand and opening the door. I hadn't been planning on going back with her, but it suddenly seems like the most natural thing in the world. I grab my jacket and we're on our way.

Tomorrow Morning

Mary Morell

Sophie watched her reflection in the mirror which was as old as she was. The six panes of mirrored glass had been set into a window frame just months before her birth in order to conserve wall space in her mother's tiny bathroom. Sophie ignored the small spider who had taken up residence between the mirror and the edge of the sink. Better than fly paper and not as messy, she thought, pulling the bristles of the brush through her short grey hair. Her mind heard echoes of her mother's words: "Use a comb on wet hair. The dampness ruins brushes." Mothers were sometimes wrong. Or perhaps it took more than sixty-two years of daily dampness. Carefully she examined the bristles of the brush she had gotten on her 10th birthday. It still had every bristle in place.

"Counting the grey hairs, Soph?" The strong low voice drew Sophie's eyes back to the mirror. Jennie's wide brown eyes crinkled with her grin.

"No, the bristles. Wondering if it will ever wear out. I'd sure hate to get used to a new one after all this time." She resumed brushing her straight thick hair. Her father's hair, so different from her mother's kinky curls. She saw Jennie reach out her hand; the strong fingers touched the nape of her neck and entwined with her hair. She made a humming sound almost like a purr.

"Now I'll just have to brush it again," she said, leaning into the beginning of a neck massage.

"Want me to stop?" Jennie asked.

"I suppose I could just brush it again. But if I'm going to do that much work you might as well mess the whole of it." Sophie grinned into the mirror.

Jennie draped a towel over the lid of the toilet. "Here, sit down and let me do it right." Her trained sure fingers began to probe the muscles of Sophie's shoulders. "Tsk," she commented, "you've been worrying again."

"About the babies. Most of these new mothers have never held a baby. How are they going to know how to raise one? I was the oldest of five children. I raised the younger ones and learned on them before I had my two."

"And were you a better mother than your younger sisters?" Jennie prodded patiently at a knot in Sophie's shoulder.

"No, but . . ."

"Give it up, Sophie. Let go of it. Things will turn out fine. These little ones are born into a world much better than ours. Every single one is wanted. There's enough food for everyone. They'll have enough grandmothers to advise their mothers. Don't worry. It's just a bad habit you won't give up." She could feel the knot loosening.

"I gave up smoking. That was enough virtue for a lifetime." Sophie relaxed into the rhythm of the massage.

"You wicked old woman. Trying to claim a virtue when you had no choice!" Her hands pulled Sophie's back to rest on her breast. "You didn't give them up until there weren't any more and then you raged around like a rabid skunk. I was there. I remember. Tell your tales of virtue to the rest of the village, but not to me, old woman." The muscles in Sophie's neck began to loosen as she allowed her head to rest safely in Jennie's hands.

Sophie laughed without reserve. "You know me too well, sweet Jennie." She closed her eyes and hummed the same tuneless song as Jennie moved her attention to Sophie's face. She worked her fingers up, away from the gravity that pulled now loosened skin downward.

"That feels wonderful."

"Shh. No talking while I work on your face. You have a wonderful face, you know. Generous lips that don't disappear like mine. I'm very envious of your lips." She pressed the tension out of the tiny muscles around Sophie's mouth so that her lips became even fuller. "This is the dangerous part of the face massage. Will I be able to be self-disciplined enough not to kiss those wonderful lips or will I throw virtue to the winds? And, as usual, wickedness wins." She held Sophie's head carefully as she bent over and grazed her lips across Sophie's.

Sophie stiffened her neck just enough to hold her head up herself and enjoy the gentle kisses that were covering every inch of her face. She put her hands on Jennie's shoulder and pulled herself to standing. "I'm too old for sex in adventuresome places. Let's go to a nice comfortable bed."

"You're just feeling old because there are babies again. You're only seventy-two and in excellent health. I should know," she said, letting Sophie pull her toward the bedroom.

"Just because you are one of many medical technicians in this village does not give you cause to put on airs, woman." She pulled Jennie onto the futon platform and began unbuttoning her robe. "Now, if you want to put on airs because you have the most talented hands in any of the five villages of Red Valley, you may feel free to do so." Sophie kissed each of Jennie's ten talented fingertips and then their palms.

"You should know, old witch, you tried out almost every one."

"Well, I was a little wild there at first. Losing almost all my family and friends made me crazy." She moved her lips up to Jennie's wrists.

"And you were one of the lucky ones with both a daughter and a granddaughter still living." She shed her robe in one graceful movement.

"Still, all that death made me crazy for sex."

"And what's your excuse now? No one you know has died in years and you are just as ready as a rabbit."

"Must be the births. Every fertile woman is pregnant. I must be feeling the pressure to breed." She kissed the inside of Jennie's elbow and lingered there.

"Unless I missed something in my training, these two old ladies are not likely to accomplish that." She slid her nakedness into the silk-lined comforter, her dark skin contrasting beautifully with the light blue. "I don't mind trying. Oh, yes, I do even like trying. But I think we'd better let the sperm banks stand until we succeed."

Sophie settled herself cross-legged on the futon, never stopping kissing Jennie's arm. She ran finger tips up and down that arm as her lips moved up the soft relaxed flesh to Jennie's shoulder.

"Of course, I never heard of a woman getting pregnant from being kissed on the arm, either." Jennie stretched into the comforter like a cat. "But please keep on trying."

The Chemistry Between Us

Ruth Mountaingrove

Max had written me she wanted to see me. We were old friends. We met when she came to my land to be part of an ever-changing collective. My partner and I were the core, and new women came into our lives for a brief three weeks and were gone. As many as a hundred women could pass through our land in a year. We got used to welcoming them with open arms, and at the end of three weeks letting them go again. Occasionally some of them stayed longer.

I welcomed Max, too. To tell you the truth, I was prepared to admire her. She was a professional into healing and had an herbal store. It was through the herbal store that she heard of our collective and wrote from the east coast that she had two weeks of vacation coming and wanted to spend it with the collective. Of course we said yes. We always said yes.

Frequently what would happen was that women would write, make elaborate arrangements, and then not show up. Other women would just come walking down our lane and into our hearts. Max flew out and arrived in a rented car. No one had to meet her. She traveled light. After the initial collective meeting she took her gear up to the cabin she had picked out for herself.

I am a photographer, so during the time she was on the land I took photographs of her with my 1904 Montgomery Ward portrait studio camera. I invited her into my darkroom to watch the negatives develop as I did all the women I photographed. I also showed her how to work in the darkroom — she had had a course in high school — and then left her to her own devices.

Nights I would hear her slipping into one of the collective women's tents and the accompanying sounds, but I ignored them, feeling that was a matter between the two of them. I must say I did wonder about her partner back east, but it really was none of my business, and when she went back they broke up.

What I didn't realize was that she was attracted to me. I was in a long term relationship which was also breaking up, but I didn't know that yet and wouldn't for a while.

Not only was she attracted to me, but she was gradually falling in love. I wondered if she would ever admit to that. Anyway, her two weeks were up and I hugged her goodbye as I did every woman. In the intensity with which we worked with each other in the collective we got very close to women, very close to heart and bone. And I loved women, opening my heart to them even while knowing they would leave.

I had been that way since I discovered how wonderful women were at the women's center back east. That discovery resulted in my becoming a lesbian two years later. It's hard to explain to someone who never lived through it what that time of awakening was like. How we loved women, every woman who came to the center. This was not eros, it was philia—sister love. It puzzled the old gays. Who was butch? Who was femme? And how come you all love each other? And why aren't you afraid? But we were never afraid. Angry, yes, because of what was done to our sisters. Angry, yes, and I remember not being depressed for a whole year. We were going to change the world women were living in. I believe we did.

So we said goodbye. She went back to her life still attracted to me and I went back to mine.

Awhile after that my world began to fall apart. I was visited by a series of physical ailments and I wrote to Max describing what was happening. She advised me to see a doctor, but I try to avoid them whenever possible, so I put it off. Eventually I did get a complete physical. By that time the ailments were under better control. And by that time my partner's and my relationship was unraveling too.

What was amazing to me at this time was that no matter how far apart we lived, Max always knew when I was going through a rough time. She would dream about me and then write to tell me of her dreams and ask how I was. Meanwhile she found another partner and was happy again, but still attracted, apparently. A couple of years later they moved to the west coast.

I, too, found another lover, several of them, and then one day when I had moved to another state and was settled in a small apartment I invited her to come for a visit. She did, promising her partner she would not touch me, a promise I had also made to my lover since I was now monogamous again. We were good. We did the right thing.

There was a terrific storm the night she left and as we hugged each other goodbye and kissed with closed lips I knew there was chemistry between us. I suggested she wait out the storm and leave in the morning, but she almost ran out of the apartment. We were good.

By the time she wrote, she had broken up with her partner and I was just out of a year-long relationship of my own. She wrote that she couldn't really take time off from her job as she had planned but she would drive up and get me and take me back for a week-long visit if I were up for it. I said I was. Mostly I don't like to travel, and my car was not in any condition to make a long trip, so my saying yes was unusual. A risk. Suppose we didn't like being together for a week. Well, I would take that chance. I had no pressing obligations. I would go.

She arrived the night of the full moon. When we hugged I could feel that same chemistry. So, I thought, it's still there. Did she feel it too? We went to get her duffle bag and other things out of her car and put them in the bedroom. Then we sat down in the kitchen to talk about our lives and drink tea. Max had just had a tarot reading and she showed me the diagrams of where the cards had been and read me the interpretations. Occasionally our hands touched, lightly, as we bent over the paper. I got out my tarot deck and we each pulled a card. The Tower for me, the World for her. Would we be compatible? Maybe.

She had written she wanted to be my cuddle buddy. That sounded good to me. I hadn't been cuddled in a long time. So after two hours of talking and drinking tea it was midnight and we decided to go to bed. It had been a long drive and she was tired. While she brushed her teeth, I cleaned up the kitchen.

My cuddle buddy rules are that you big spoon with your clothes on, not fully dressed, but pjs or a long tee shirt and panties. So that's what we wore.

We got into bed, turned out the light and Max put her arms around me and sighed. How could I resist that? I turned in her arms and kissed her.

Max said with such passion that her voice shook, "I don't really want to cuddle you. I want to make love to you, but I will do whatever you say."

Well, I had known we were going to be lovers the night of the storm when she didn't stay. That night Max had kept us good. Given the choice between cuddling and making love there was no contest, so we took off our clothes and tossed them on the floor.

She said, holding me in her arms, "I have wanted you so long!" Then she kissed me and all the longing between us turned into fire. She was a fierce lover and I met that fierceness with my own. Her thigh riding my fire, we came together after all those years of wanting and waiting. Afterwards she kept saying "I didn't think it would be so good. I didn't think it could be so good." Yes, we were good.

We slept and woke to explore each other with fingers, with tongues, with fingertip tracings around the ears, across the eyebrows, down the bridge of the nose, around the mouth, down the neck, across the shoulders, around the breasts, down the back, spiraling around and around, adding fire to fire. We danced together on my bright orange sheets in the full moon streaming in the window.

The next morning we left for her house in San Francisco. It was a long trip and the first thing that Max suggested, when we arrived, was a bath. This was after she had shown me her Victorian house and the guest room where I was to sleep. She ran the water into the claw-footed tub and called me when the bath was ready. How good that water felt. I washed my hair and my body slowly, sensuously, and she came in and gently poured water over my head and down my back. I stretched out in the marvelously long bath tub and totally relaxed.

After my bath I walked into the bedroom. Max had lit a candle and its shadow was flickering on the wall. She had turned down the covers.

I got into bed, sliding between the sheets, and looked around the room. There was my guitar and my camera, my journal next to the candle, my suitcase on the floor. There was also a wicker bookcase with some books Max had selected for the guest room, her clarinet, some games, a chess set. There was a round Japanese rice paper lamp shade over the ceiling fixture, shedding a warm glow.

Max came in from her bath. Was she going to sleep here or in her own bed? I waited, unsure of what she might decide to do now that she was in her own home. She had no such problem. She came straight to the bed, got in under the covers and kissed me. And began a slow, tender love making, nibbling my ear, kissing my throat, my breasts, my navel, my inner thighs, while I traced swirls and lines on her back, under her armpit, kissed and sucked her fingers one by one.

Every lover I have ever had has made love differently. Max's love making was radical. It transformed me at the root. Cellular transformation is what I called it; every cell in my body responded to her touch. The tarot card I pulled from the tarot pack was correct. I was transformed.

My fingers learned her body. My mouth learned her breasts. And I learned the connection between her breasts and the walls of her cave as it gripped my fingers and she arched her back and came screaming.

Who was butch? Who was femme? Who was top? Who was bottom? We took turns as desire moved us. I enjoy giving pleasure. I enjoy receiving it.

What more can I tell you? Max showed me her city. We had lunch with some of her friends. I also had friends in the city. I visited them while she worked. We made love in that room and the walls rang with our passion.

We did not become a couple. We did not move in together. I had a life and a goal I was pursuing and so did she. For a while we thought we might continue as lovers, but distance defeated us as it has many women.

We are back to being friends. She says I changed her life. She certainly changed mine. And the tarot card she pulled that night of the full moon — the World — was prophetic. She is half way around the world now, seeking and finding a divine love and peace.

And me? I haven't had a new lover since Max. She was all I ever wanted, but I was unwilling to give up my life to be with her. If I had, that would have been a different story, wouldn't it?

The Dinner Guest

Winn Gilmore

Rain drummed against the windows like a lover's insistent fingers. Opal rose as languorous as a cat and turned off the stereo relaying the perky newscaster's voice announcing that "Rain, ladies and gentlemen, is expected to continue 'till late tomorrow evening, and flooding has already been reported in Sonoma County." She put on an album and stood with her arms wrapped around herself as Anita Baker's voice poured thick as sweet, warm honey through the living room.

The telephone lines had gone down an hour ago. She worried that Mollika had tried in vain to notify her that no, she couldn't possibly reach Opal's house in the downpour.

She rested her left cheek against the cool, uncaring windowpane and closed her eyes. The light from the fireplace's dancing flames splashed frescoes inside her closed lids. Of all nights for it to rain, she thought hotly. She had survived the week with the promise of tonight's date tucked deep inside her like butterscotch sucked secretly, slowly between the tongue and roof of her mouth. After a particularly grueling day, she would reward herself with fantasies of this night, rolling the sweet candy of desire from the left to the right side of her mouth, then back to the left. She swallowed.

Damn! The avocadoes would rot, turn brown, and suck in on themselves from disuse. The mangoes would metamorphose into sour, shrivelled things odious to the sight.

It doesn't really matter, she chided herself. She jerked her face away from the windowpane as if it burned. She's not coming. I know it. At least I tried.

Actually, she was relieved. Over the past two years she'd taken a long, arduous voyage away from herself. She'd swum the treacherous waters of white women's souls and bodies, diving deeper into them and further away from herself each time she dipped her thirsty tongue between their golden legs. She'd imagined that she was inhaling knowledge and sustenance from that never-ending river, when actually she'd been breathing HER life and spirit into THEM. So, she was relieved that Mollika, with thick locks swaying, would not come tonight. Now she could get on with the business of trying to lose herself between white women's thighs. She decided to take another bath.

She slipped slowly into the almost-too-hot water, skin prickling deliciously, vaginal muscles tightening, then opening, as she acclimatized. She drew up her knees and the water covered her full, brown breasts, nipples sticking out adamantly like twin islands from the sea. She ran her fingers over her still-flat belly and down to her water-loosened curls floating like sea flowers over the ocean's bottom. Her mouth opened and eyes closed as she found her clitoris, then her slippery lips. She was pleasantly surprised at the slick wetness there, and the fingers of her right hand slipped up and down, in and out, of her pussy. She shivered and murmured, "Mollika."

What is this? she thought angrily, and began washing herself. Still, when she stepped out of the water, she couldn't deny the full, wet clit that her thirsty towel found. She spread her legs and leaned against the wall. Her pelvis rocked forward to meet her hand. She moaned.

The doorbell rang.

Her heart leapt and her mouth went dry as she hurriedly dried herself. A part of her wanted to rush to the door just as she was, naked and hungry for the other woman. "Just a minute!" she yelled as she stepped into her caftan.

"Sorry I'm late," Mollika said, grinning. "This rain, you know."

Opal knew she could drown in this woman's smile spread wide over her face, with big, beautiful teeth shining forth a much-needed promise.

"Oh, that's alright. Come on in," she said, pulling back from the precipice. "I was in the bathtub."

"Yeah, I can tell," Mollika laughed, wiping suds from Opal's forehead. I wish I'd been in there with you, she thought.

Opal's rebellious nipples tightened, and she took Mollika's soaked raincoat. "Why don't you dry yourself in front of the fire?" she asked, looking away. I've got to control this, she reminded herself. I hardly know this woman. "You're wet."

"To the bone," Mollika added, smiling slyly. She bent in front of the fire, shaking her dreadlocks like a horse its mane.

Opal took in the woman's full buttocks with no hint of panty line, and hung the coat in the hall. "I didn't think you'd make it," she said from that safe distance. "It IS raining hard."

"Yeah, girl, but you know, there's something about the rain. When I was a little bitty girl," Mollika said, squinching up her face and holding her right thumb and forefinger together to show just how small, "I used to sneak out of the house and stand in the rain. I'd run around in circles with my arms thrown out, head held high and mouth open to catch the drops. It just does something to me."

"Sounds dangerous," Opal said, walking back into the living room. "You could've been struck by lightning."

Mollika laughed hard and said, "Yep, guess I always have lived dangerously. Some things never change."

Opal frowned. "Well, I hope you're hungry."

"As a bear."

"Good. I made a big dinner."

They started with the avocadoes, so perfect that Mollika moaned when her lips wrapped around her first bite. "Ummmm, if this is any indication of things to come . . ."

Opal blushed, wondering whether her guest meant the food or something more. She half-hoped, half-feared she meant something more. "Well, I think you'll like it," she said recklessly. For the first time, she looked directly into Mollika's eyes.

They laughed and talked their way through wok vegetables, home-made bread, and potato pie. They smiled so much, Opal thought her face would break.

Mollika insisted on doing the dishes and Opal watched, engrossed, as the suds lapped up her guest's strong black arms. Her fingers caressed each dish, and Opal wished the hands were soaping her.

Mollika looked at the woman's elbow resting on the counter, chin in hand, caftan open just enough to reveal the promise of what lay hidden within. She touched one sudsy finger to Opal's chest and trailed it to the woman's face. She moved closer to Opal, who lifted her face imploringly.

Opal slid her body into Mollika's, drinking in the smell of rain that still hovered about her guest's body, fresh and moist. She slid one hand up Mollika's back, and Mollika shook, pulling Opal even closer. As Opal's nipples, then breasts, pushed against her, Mollika took in the slightly parted mouth, teeth glistening wet, tongue pressed between them. She pressed her lips against Opal's and groaned as the woman's tongue leapt into her mouth. She sucked her in, then gave herself in return.

Opal was aflame, her clit tightening spasmodically. It's been so long, she thought. She held tight to Mollika's dreads, fingers climbing up the ropes to her skull. She pulled away and looked deep into Mollika's beckoning eyes, then led the way to the bedroom.

"Girl, I sure hope you're not bisexual," Mollika whispered, only half-kiddingly, before her tongue circled into Opal's ear.

"Not at all," Opal moaned, her tongue and lips blazing a path over and down Mollika's left breast. "Why?"

As Opal's lips, then teeth, clamped around her nipple, Mollika murmured, "You never know what you'll pick up. You know?"

"Um-hmmmmm."

Mollika sank to her knees and ran her hands down Opal's legs. The bed looming behind, she lifted Opal's caftan. She kissed her way up one leg, inhaling the warm bathtub-and-sex scent.

Opal cried out and sank her fingers into Mollika's hair to steady herself. She couldn't still her trembling legs, and she pushed her pussy outward, begging Mollika to love her.

"What's wrong?" Mollika teased, hovering over the other woman's opening. Though her fingers only played around the edges of Opal's clit, she could feel the heat, the wetness, radiating like flames from the living room fire. "You want something, no?"

Opal tried to pull away, to erect walls to protect herself from this unknown teaser. You'd better run now, before she steals your heart, your very spirit, her brain screamed. She could hurt you like no white woman ever could. But her pussy was screaming another, more insistent, message. She burned for Mollika's touch, for her fingers to be lodged deep within her. Still, she managed to pull away.

"No," Mollika pleaded. "What're you running from? This?" And her lips wrapped around Opal's clit. Opal moaned and fell back onto the bed. Mollika lifted her and slowly raised the caftan, kissing each morsel of flesh exposed.

Opal helped Mollika out of her clothes, marvelling at the skin smooth and brown as her own. She pulled Mollika down with her, kissing first her mouth, then her neck, and down finally to her nipples. Mollika slid down Opal's body. Opal opened her legs and welcomed her sister, her lover, to find solace there, to rock her soul and satisfy her thirst.

"My guest," Opal whispered, smooth as silk, "do you like it?"

Mollika lingered at Opal's navel, inhaling the earthy musk layering her lover's body. Her tongue was water over stone, sluicing down, down into Opal's juices flowing between her legs. She grazed the pubic hair nestling Opal's pussy. Opal twisted her hips and, grabbing a lock, said, "No."

"No?" Mollika parroted, unbelieving. She moved back up to Opal's face. Her fingers danced around Opal's clit, itching to slide slowly, surely, inside her. "Why not? Let me taste you, like this," Mollika begged as she licked and sniffed Opal's armpit. "And suck you, like this." She drew hard on her lover's nipple. "And kiss you, like this." She darted her tongue into Opal's mouth, the tip undulating in loose circles. She felt Opal's body relax, and she slid down to her sex.

Mollika wrapped her mouth around Opal's lips and exhaled gently, then drew in the heady scent of moss and thick vegetation covering the earth. Like a kneeling woodswoman tilling the earth with her fingers, she parted Opal's hair. Her mouth watered when she beheld the deep pink nestled within Opal's brown lips. Finally, she dived.

Her flattened tongue licked the surface of Opal's clit, and Opal's legs opened wider. Mollika wet a finger with Opal's juices and trailed it up to pinch one nipple. "Yes," Opal moaned. "Yes." Mollika's tongue traveled deeper into her.

Opal wrapped her legs around Mollika's back. Her juices flowed like a freshly tapped well as the roar gathered within her. Her whole skin prickled as Mollika slipped one long black arm beneath her, lifting her sex. Opal moaned, "So soon?"

The dam burst, sending wave after crashing wave through her body. Her legs tightened around Mollika and her body flowed up, up, up to meet the lips, tongue, and teeth of the woman who'd brought her home.

When the waves subsided, Mollika kissed Opal's clit, then blazed a path up to her mouth. Opal smiled into Mollika's sex-wet face. "Welcome home, guest," she said.

Blue

Terri de la Peña

I can see the stars through the open hatch of Blue's van. In the haze over Los Angeles, they are rarely visible. There only the pearly moon shines through smog-tinged skies, its radiance dimmed by trendy neon and ubiquitous headlights. But in Yosemite, I have a chance to view nature's midnight show, and I stare into its flickering canopy, reveling in that silent awesomeness.

Blue does not stir. On her back she sleeps, her big body slack against the wide mattress, one muscled arm outside the faded patchwork quilt. In the sliver of moonlight, I notice again that her skin is nearly as brown as mine. Her tan results from a vigorous outdoor existence; mine is natural.

I snuggle deeper within the quilt, feeling Blue's radiating heat. Hefty women are more reliable than flannel sheets or insulated sleeping bags. Often more lovable, too, I remind myself. What a long lonely time since I've made love with a big woman. And, looking up once more, I wink at the stars, wondering if I dare.

* * * * *

In the swirling dust of the Music Festival's parking area, I spotted her unmistakable form. She wore a fluorescent orange vest, khaki shorts, a Stetson with an eagle feather hooked into its crown, and a red bandanna tied outlaw-style below her Ray-Bans. With a shrill whistle, she waved her thick arms towards the oncoming traffic.

I gasped, not only in recognizing her, but also in glimpsing her bare breasts poking through the vest. I liked how they swung while she moved with assurance; they were so much paler than the rest of her. I remembered the many times she had sneaked behind me and grabbed mine, pressing her large ones into my back. She always stopped when I responded to her fondling, satisfied at arousing me. We were amigas para siempre—never lovers.

Despite the billowing dust, I cranked my window lower and leaned out. "Órale. Tienes chichis magníficos, mujer."

She did a slow double-take before breaking into a grin. "Is that you, Chica?"

"The one and only."

"Chic Lozano!" With her open palm, Blue slammed the hood of my VW. "It's been ages, girl. You're lookin' good."

"You, too." I let my eyes linger. "Where do I park?"

"By those trees. Wait for me, huh? My shift's almost over. I'll help you get settled."

* * * * *

I glance at the stars, fascinated by the night's still brilliance. Earlier Blue and I had sat side by side among the hundreds of women gathered in the natural amphitheater; we seemed the only ones half-listening to Lucie Blue Tremblay sing of lovers past and present.

"Pues, que pasó?" I whispered, leaning against Blue's sturdy shoulder. "When you left with her for Oregon . . ."

"You thought it'd last?" Her short wavy hair hugged the sides of her broad Scotch-Irish face. "So did I, babe. So did I." She watched me for a moment, her blue-grey eyes steady. "And you?"

I shrugged. "Mine left me for a black woman. I guess I just wasn't dark enough."

Blue turned to stare before her eyes crinkled, and I laughed first. She nudged me, pulling me closer. "So it's just you and me again, Chica."

"Yeah. Like old times." I rested my head against the scratchy wool of her Pendleton jacket. "You planning to stay in Oregon?"

She nodded. "Bought land there. Hey, girl—the city life was never for me. You know that. Drive up to see me soon."

"I'd like that."

* * * * *

When she saw my flimsy tent, Blue insisted I stay with her in the van. At first I grumbled—after all, I had come to the Music Festival to get used to being solo again. Always eager to rescue me, Blue claimed I made her feel maternal. Sometimes I wondered if my being Chicana awakened her nostalgia as well.

Born and raised in Tucson, she spoke some Spanish; her first lover had been Chicana, too. Whatever Blue's reasons, I knew she genuinely cared for me, and she had a strange way of appearing whenever I felt most vulnerable.

During the concert, when the valley's temperature dropped to a level too cold for my southern Californian bones to tolerate, I became grateful for Blue's offer. She kept one arm around me, occasionally fingering my cheek, as if assuring herself of my presence. I kept my head against her, my hand in hers.

"Am I still the only one who calls you 'Chica?'"

I raised my head and smiled. "No one else has the nerve."

"You got pretty feisty the first time I said it."

"Thought you were putting me down."

She poured me a cup of Irish coffee from her ever-ready thermos. "Jumping to conclusions, as usual, Lozano."

I took the drink and savored it, letting the coffee slowly slide down my throat. "At least you figured out 'Chic' comes from 'Francisca.'"

"And since you were such a cute baby dyke, I just had to dub you 'Chica.'"

I grinned, signaling for another cupful. "I've missed you, Blue."

She clicked her cup to mine. "Ditto. Never figured I'd see you here, especially without what's-her-name. That woman must've been crazy, babe."

"Yeah. Like yours."

* * * * * *

The heavens continue to sparkle while Blue sleeps. Beneath the quilt, I reach for her warm hand, caressing its strong contours. I remember the first time I felt those now-familiar fingers.

She had seen me in the bar, hanging by the pool table, watching the others play. A scrawny kid, I stayed on the sidelines, too shy to approach anyone. And Blue appeared suddenly, cue in hand, her grin wide and friendly. Before I knew it, she took my hand, guiding my fingers into position, teaching me how to hold the cue. She spent that whole evening teasing me, making me laugh, welcoming me into her world.

She has known me longer than most, but never completely. I wonder why. In the darkness, I stare at her. She is a country dyke, bold and self-sufficient. Her hand, big and calloused from outdoor chores, attests to this.

I lie on my side, studying her. Very slowly, careful not to wake her, I begin to guide her rugged hand over me, remembering her gentle touch on my cheek earlier. Through the tee shirt my nipple tightens when her palm brushes against it, and I shiver at the fleeting sensation. I smile, imagining what I will do if she awakens. And I realize then that I want her to open her eyes, to touch me deliberately.

I bring her hand to my lips, lightly kissing each fingertip. Several times I repeat this, and eventually I hear a low moan escape her lips. Before long, her fingers outline my mouth, and I suck them within, tasting their saltiness.

"Ay, Chica," she murmurs. "I thought I was dreaming."

"Nope. Not jumping to conclusions, either."

She raises her brows at my answer. "Hey, girl—"

"Blue, why not? We've both thought about it."

She considers that briefly. "Look, I'm not moving back to L.A."

"Don't expect you to. And Oregon's not ready for me."

She looks serious. "We'll still be friends?"

"Always."

We smile at each other then, and I cuddle against her. Soon I raise my tee and rub my breasts against hers. She pulls me closer, all the while unbuttoning her flannel shirt. In seconds, her mouth surrounds mine, our tongues sensuously meeting. We kiss for ages, shedding our clothes in the process. I cling to her and gasp with pleasure when she eases me onto her.

My hands roam over her large body, delighting in its abundance. She is so much bigger than me, her breasts twice the size of mine, her rounded belly and thighs a pleasurable cushion for my more angular body. I spread myself over her and rub my face over her breasts, licking first one nipple, then the other. I remember how her breasts had swung beneath the fluorescent vest, and that image arouses me further. I bite one nipple.

She begins to groan, and when she does, I move back and crouch over her, offering my own breasts. She takes one into her mouth, and I marvel how it fits so easily. I lean forward and close my eyes, luxuriating in that sensation. And she finds my tuft, her fingers barely tracing my clitoris, then slipping inside. I quiver, gasping again when her fingers enter further. She keeps them there, her mouth remaining at my breast.

I raise myself and straddle her, and she lets go of my breast with a sudden slurping sound. We both laugh at this. The amusement on her face slackens, though, when I reach inside her. She licks her lips in anticipation and watches me with a longing I have never seen on her familiar face. She lifts one hand to cup my breast, pinching my nipple. I lean back to enjoy her fondling, her strong fingers exploring me.

And my hand probes her endlessly. She is so roomy; my whole hand could fit here. Blue moans when I tantalizingly rub myself against her, grinding my hips into her while keeping my fingers within. She slips her fingers out then, gliding them upwards to my clit. I breathe quickly at her sudden touch, her calloused thumb provoking me.

"Remember when I used to stick my hands in your front pockets and jiggle my fingers?" she whispers.

"It made me crazy, like now. Always thought you were playing with me . . . "

"I'm not, Chica. I want you."

"I want you, too, Blue."

My other hand lazily locates her clitoris, circling it, covering it, teasing it. She makes a guttural sound, and I look at her, eyes half open, wavy hair mussed, her big body caught in my rhythm. I shiver a bit from the open hatch, but the heat she exudes warms me. Playfully, our vaginas gurgle to each other, and we laugh again, increasing our circular motions, breathing in excited unison. Our bodies, so different in color and shape, blend together perfectly.

Blue comes before me, growling, tossing her head, her thighs flexing abruptly. And then, without missing a beat, she turns me over, licking, sucking, making me dizzy enough to be in orbit, floating among the constellations. I sweat and moan, nearly crying, almost laughing, my legs wrapped around her broad shoulders. A burly mountain woman makes wild love to me, and I come with a fury, the moon and stars colliding with my whirling body.

Blue holds me tightly, murmuring nonsense. "Muy picante. I want another taste of your salsa."

Smiling, I lie breathless within her arms. After some moments, I meet her bemused eyes. "Hey, Blue—what's your address in Oregon, anyway?"

Contributors

Julie Blackwomon

Julie Blackwomon, a working class poet and fiction writer, most recently has been anthologized in *Women's Glib* and *Lesbian Bedtime Stories II*. She is the author of a book of poetry, *Revolutionary Blues and Other Fevers*, and co-author of a book of short fiction, *Voyages 2*.

I see "Maggie, Sex, and the Baby Jesus, Too" as not so much an erotic piece as a gentle nudging at the boundaries of acceptable humor. It was inspired by a snatch of conversation I overheard at a women's music festival. It has given me great pleasure to discover that women find it sexy as well as humorous. I had fun writing it.

Maureen Brady

Maureen Brady, author of *Give Me Your Good Ear*, *Folly*, and *The Question She Put To Herself*, has received grants from the Ludwig Vogelstein Foundation, The Barbara Deming Memorial Fund, CAPS, and the New York State Council on the Arts writer-in-residence program. She teaches writing workshops at the Crystal Quilt in N.Y.C. and the Resource Center for Accessible Living in Kingston, N.Y. She is presently completing her novel, *Rocking Bone Hollow*, and a book of meditations for women sexual abuse survivors, *Daybreak*, to be released by Hazelden/Harper in October 1991. She was born June 7, 1943 in Mt. Vernon, New York, graduated from the University of Florida in 1965 and received her M.A. from N.Y.U.

One of the focuses of her writing over the past several years has been sexuality and its meaning to her characters. She has written stories about incest and stories about women coming to knowledge about themselves through their erotic reachings. She is interested in the connections between sexuality and spirituality and how women struggle to claim their own natures, frequently after having been robbed in childhood.

Beth Brant

Beth Brant is a Bay Of Quinte Mohawk from Tyendinaga Mohawk Territory in Ontario. She is the editor of *A Gathering of Spirit*, a collection of writing and art by Native American women (Firebrand Books, 1989). She is the author of *Mohawk Trail*, prose and poetry (Firebrand Books, 1985) and *Food & Spirits*, short fiction (Firebrand Books, 1991). Her work had appeared in numerous Native and Feminist anthologies and she has done readings, lectures, and taught creative writing throughout

North America. She currently lives in Michigan and is a lesbian mother and grandmother.

I wrote this poem as I was in Vancouver and missing my lover, Denise, who was back home in Michigan. I wanted to conjure up for myself the images of her body and making love to her. I was very lonely for her!! I have rarely written about sex/love without thinking of her. This poem was also a gift to her for the love she has shared with me.

Tee A. Corinne

I was born 11/3/43 in St. Petersburg, Florida, grew up in Florida and North Carolina, and spent significant time in the Carribean as a teen. My primary identity is as an artist. I work at writing. I have a B.A. from the U. of South Florida (major in art, minors in history and literature) and a M.F.A. in art from Pratt Institute. My books include *The Cunt Coloring Book, Lovers,* and *Dreams of the Woman Who Loved Sex.* I edited *Intricate Passions,* a Lambda Literary Award winning collection of erotic writing.

As a person who is mildly dyslexic, for whom grammar is often elusive and spelling a disaster, the fact that my writing is even published continues to surprise the child in me. I write erotica out of a need to read and share my own kind of story—not high drama sex or wildly acrobatic sex—rather warm, comforting, garden-variety sex that nourishes year after year.

Emma Joy Crone

Born on the 19th January, 1928, Manchester, England where I grew up and remained until the age of 39. My formal education terminated at the age of 15. At 40 I became a student of life, immigrating to New York, then living in San Francisco where I encountered feminism and lesbian love.

Now 23 years and many relationships later I live in Canada on one of the Gulf Islands off British Columbia.

At 60 I discovered my writing self, and following the publication of "Comments of a Working Class Crone" in *Fireweed* (a Feminist Quarterly) I was inspired to put together a newsletter, *A Web of Crones,* designed to increase the visibility of older lesbian/political/spiritual women. After 4 years doing it alone, *A Web* combined with *Visible* (Mendocino) for which I still write. My poetry and articles have appeared in *Testimonies,* a collection of lesbian coming-out stories, *Amazones D'Hier/ Lesbiennes D'Aujourd'Hui, B.O.A.* (Bevy of Anarchists), *Maize* (a country lesbian magazine), and *Diversity* (a lesbian rag of Vancouver, B.C.).

I wrote about sensuality and sexuality because I enjoy both. I wanted to acknowledge them as ecstatic and joyous parts of my life and to free myself from old inhibitions. I'm now enjoying sharing my 63rd year with my 35 year old lover. Rest assured, old women never dry up—

IF one has an active sex life. I did (dry up) in the midst of celibacy and my woman gynecologist said "masturbate."

Terri de la Peña

Writing this short bio seems like deja vu since I also have a story in Tee's *Intricate Passions*. Rather than repeat details, here is an update. My stories appear in *Lesbian Bedtime Stories*, Vols. 1 and 2; *Finding Courage: Stories by Women; The One You Call Sister; Word of Mouth: Short-Short Stories by Women; Finding the Lesbians: Personal Accounts from Around the World;* the Chicana issue of *Frontiers: A Journal of Women's Studies;* and more are forthcoming in *Lesbian Love Stories* Vol. 2, and in *Chicana Lesbians* (Third Woman Press). My novel *Margins* is forthcoming from The Seal Press in 1992.

I continue focusing my fiction on Chicanas, lesbians or otherwise. As Gloria Anzaldúa says, "Being a mestiza queer person, una de las otras, is living in a lot of worlds, some of which overlap." I aim to explore this shifting territory through stories like "Blue," where, despite cultural and physical differences, Chic Lozano stretches the borders of friendship. Presenting this fictional erotic encounter between a Chicana and a white woman, portraying their relationship in a non-manipulative manner, is one of my attempts to bridge that gap often existing between mujeres de color and other lesbians. And whenever I delve into the emotional dynamics between women, I find it impossible to ignore their sexuality. De eso no se hable—so I write about it instead.

Natalie Devora

I am an African-American Albino woman, born in Oakland, California on July 22, 1962. I grew up in Oakland and attended Holy Names College. I have earned a bachelors degree in psychology from San Francisco State University. I have studied writing with Gloria Anzaldua, editor of *This Bridge Called My Back* and *Borderlands/La Frontera* and with Cherríe Moraga, author of *Loving In The War Years* and co-editor of *This Bridge Called My Back*. I have had work published in *Sinister Wisdom* #38 and *Aché*, a journal for lesbians of African descent. I am also published under a pseudonym in *The Courage To Heal* written by Laura Davis and Ellen Bass.

I write erotica because I want to be able to freely express my sexuality. I want to offer qualitative sex writing to a community that hungers for it. I want to be known as a radical, for I talk about sex.

Ayofemi Folayan

An activist concerned with saving our planet and creating a world of peace and harmony, Ayofemi Folayan pursues the end of all forms of violence and oppression through her creative energy as a writer. An Aries who hails originally from the East Coast, her work has been anthologized in *In A Different Light, An Anthology of Lesbian Writers, Spring Street,*

Lesbians at Midlife: The Creative Transition, Indivisible, and *Blood Whispers.* Her columns, essays, book reviews and short fiction have appeared in *Gay Community News, Matrix, BLK, off our backs, Sojourner, Vanguard,* and *The Advocate.* A performance artist and crossword puzzle addict, Ayofemi is currently working on a new performance piece, "The Talking Drum," and finishing her novel, *Onyx.*

This is my virgin exploration of erotic writing. It is important to me not to exclude the realm of fantasy and self-pleasuring from collections of this kind. For many lesbians, including me, this is still the only active sex life possible, whether because there is a history of sexual abuse or assault or because there is presently no partner available or because of choosing celibacy. I hope this opens yet another closet door for other writers who have similar tales to tell.

Carolyn Gage

I was born in 1952 in Richmond, Virginia, where I attended a private school for girls. I currently live in Ashland, Oregon, where I work as a lesbian/feminist playwright and direct productions for No To Men, a radical lesbian theatre company. I tour with my one-woman show, *The Second Coming of Joan of Arc,* and have had my work published in *Trivia, Sinister Wisdom,* and several short story anthologies.

My erotica is a rehearsal space for me. It's impossible to experience what one cannot envision, and women waste a good deal of time politically and personally, climbing on the stage of experience before we have put in the necessary time with the script: envisioning the scene, identifying the obstacles, focusing our intentions. Our culture is deliberately lacking in woman-identified sexual role models—and especially models which address how a sexually traumatized woman, which most of us are, can reclaim her body. I write erotica to set the stage for my next step in reclaiming.

Rocky Gámez

I was born and raised in the lower Rio Grande Valley of Texas where most of my short stories take place. I live and work in the San Francisco Bay Area and have been a contributor to a number of anthologies, among them *Cuentos by Latinas, Conditions, Politics of the Heart, Wayward Girls and Wicked Women, Women on Women,* and *Intricate Passions.*

Writing lesbian erotica has never been my cup of tea, however, how can I refuse the invitation of a dear friend such as Tee Corinne? Like Rocky in "A Matter of Fact," this writer is still very shy about sexual matters, but my character "Gloria" is definitely not, and most of the time I have to forget my inhibitions and allow her to be who she is. To deny her this part of her character would be like denying her the core of her existence, since that *is* what propels her into all her misadventures. I have known the real Gloria for many many years and my feeling is that as long as she continues to be functional in this area of her inexhaustible expertise, she will continue to give me enough material for my stories. "A Matter of Fact" is, indeed, a matter of fact.

Winn Gilmore
I was born in New York, grew up in Alabama, went to college in Massachusetts, and now I live in California. I love words, women, fishing, and martial arts, though not necessarily in that order. I've been published in the magazines *Aché* and *On Our Backs*, the journal *Sinister Wisdom*, and the anthologies *Unholy Alliances* and *Herotica II*. My first short story collection, *Trip To Nawlins*, will be published this year (I hope).

Elissa Goldberg
I was born in May, 1961, in Dekalb, Illinois, and I grew up in Denver, Colorado. I now live in Portland, Oregon, and work as a social worker in a nursing home. I've been writing short stories for four years and will have two other pieces published this year. One story will be in an anthology of lesbian short fiction, edited by Tina Portillo, published by Alyson Press, due out in June, 1991. The other will be printed in *Word of Mouth*, vol. II, a collection of short-short stories by women, edited by Irene Zahava, published by Crossing Press, October, 1991.

"Wednesday, 7:15 a.m." is the first erotic short story I've ever written, and I wrote it mostly to see if I actually could. I found that working on it, even just sitting in front of my computer screen, was in itself erotic. It meant finding the right word for the movement I wanted. Some words push you, others draw you in, hold you, stop or release your breath. They might even be perfectly ordinary words that you'd hear anywhere on the street, but you can pull on their texture and rhythm, place them in exact spots to create just the response you want. The scariest part of writing this story was having other people read it, showing people what I consider to be erotic. When I brought it to my writing group, they giggled a lot. When I showed it to my lover, she was real quiet. The whole process has been another way for me to come out, as a lesbian, as a writer, as a person who breathes in the sensuousness of life.

Amanda Hayman
I was born on December 6th, 1951, which makes me a Sagittarian Cat, a combination I've always been particularly satisfied with. Until 1981 I lived in Great Britain, and then, in the space of a year, I moved to Japan and came out as a lesbian, both apparently on impulse. I've had articles and stories published in a variety of places, including *Lesbian Bedtime Stories*, *Serious Pleasure*, *The Original Coming Out Stories*, *off our backs*, *Trouble and Strife*, and *D. . . Dyke*, the English-language Lesbian newsletter in Japan. I wrote my first piece of fiction, a sexually explicit

short story entitled "The Flame," on a warm Thursday night in May 1987, and became so enamored with story-telling that I haven't stopped since. I am at present involved in serious relationships with the six main characters of my Lesbian novel, which is set in Anglesey, a magical island off the north coast of Wales.

I like to think of my story "Across the Straits of Georgia" as sensually explicit, a term coined by Julia Penelope. I feel that 'erotic' is too full of innuendo and nuances, and too potentially explosive, given the wide range of material it can be applied to. I think there is a place in Lesbian literature for writing about our sexual and sensual experiences, but as yet we are still feeling our way regarding the ethics of when, and where, and how, and who gets to decide what is O.K.

Terri L. Jewell

I was born October 4, 1954, in Louisville, KY. The most important facts about me now are that I'm Black, a Lesbian Feminist, and a writer. My work has appeared widely in the Lesbian, Feminist, and gay presses here and abroad since the 1980's. At present, I am co-editing *Sister Blood: Creative Writings by Black Lesbians* and compiling material for *Dread Woman/ Lock Sister*, a book by and about Black women who choose to wear dreadlocks. I will soon begin to work on my first chapbook of poetry, *And They Counted Our Teeth*.

"The Comet Watchers" is not only my first erotic fiction ever written, but is only my second piece of fiction, period! I was challenged to present Black women outside the usual stereotypes of what is sensual. I also wished to show that the sexual experience could (and does, indeed!) vary widely among women. No one can dictate sexual "propriety" despite past "emotional damage" assumed or ethereal promises of "true" self-fulfillment. We women must be aware of the conditioning that persistently imposes upon us. Each woman must decide what SHE wants and from WHOM she wants sex and HOW she wishes to receive and give sexual pleasure and satisfaction. That which is one woman's discomfort is undoubtedly another woman's passion!

Mary "Midgett" Midgett

Mary "Midgett" Midgett was born August 4, 1936, in Boston, Massachusetts. She received her AA in Early Childhood Education from CCSF and her BA in Education and Communications from Antioch University. Writings published: *Onyx* (1983), a Black women's newsletter; *Brown on Brown* (1987), African-American lesbian erotica. She is in two lesbian safe sex videos: "5 women and Masturbation" and "Latex and Lace." She is also in "Black Lesbian Erotica, 1990" and "Hot Sexposium in 1991" about fun and fantasy with sex toys. Her cassette "Body to Body" focuses on sexual relationships of the African-American Lesbian. Since 1982 she has been a "presenter-in-residence" on Human Sexuality at San Francisco State University.

I write, share, and distribute my work throughout the country because there is a limited amount of erotic literature about the African American Lesbian. Through the work — which is biofiction — I want people to know we have families and a history.

Mary Morell

On March 1, 1945 in McAllen, Texas, Mary Morell was born in the middle of a four no trump bridge hand (vulnerable, doubled and redoubled). After making her bid, Merium Morell proceeded to have six other children, bringing the family total of children to nine. At eighteen, Mary was delighted to accept the offer of a room at Our Lady of the Lake College which she had to share with only one other person. She learned in Moral Theology that writing poetry looked, to the professor, like taking notes and her writing career was begun. Her other careers included dorm mother (until being fired for being a loud mouth dyke), travel agent (until deregulation) and currently, feminist bookseller. She writes in cahoots with her partner Anne Frost and receives absolutely no assistance from men, cats, dogs or horses. If you like this story, read *Final Session*, her prizewinning novel from Spinsters.

There are layers and layers of my reasons to write about sex. First is the technical challenge. The language of sex in our society has been bankrupted by pornography and I am intrigued at the possibility of helping to create a new genre of writing. Our heritage of Puritanism has done a similar job of destroying any discussion of other pleasures. Re-reading Chaucer, I am inspired to write about swiving (mutual sexual pleasuring). I also find it a psychological challenge. I do not believe we can live a life we cannot imagine so I enjoy imagining a sexuality without the traumas of the patriarchy. Most of my other reasons are both intimate and private. I rather enjoy keeping them that way.

Ruth Mountaingrove

I was born in Philadelphia the night of a blizzard on February 21, 1923 at 7:45 pm through the intervention of forceps by a doctor known as "the butcher." My mother's doctor was playing golf in Florida but expected to be back in time for my birth. Obviously I've been a nonconformist from the start. My work has been published in *WomanSpirit*, *The Blatant Image: a magazine of feminist photography*, and in *off our backs*, *Common Lives/Lesbian Lives*, *Lesbian Ethics*, *Lesbian Contradictions*, *Gay Community News*, *Crazy Quilt*, among other publications. I have a love story in *Cats and their Dykes*, and while I have written erotic love poetry, "The Chemistry Between Us" is my first lesbian erotic short story. I have an MA in Art.

Adrienne Rich has said that we need to share our lives and our stories with each other. It is the way to build our culture and our herstory. The erotic is a part of our lives, and a part to be shared. Even

Contributor's Notes

in fiction it is a way to make ourselves real to each other. That is why I write.

Ní Aódagaín

I am a white Lesbian separatist, age 33, an incest survivor, and a writer/editor. Between raising a daughter (age 7), home schooling, and being an active community member of Oregon Women's Land (OWL) in Southern Oregon, where we live, I have managed to both have a relationship and write about that experience. As wimmin loving wimmin, we will confront more and more often the realities and difficulties of partnering as incest survivors. It is important for us to share this most sensitive and challenging aspect of our lives.

Mona Oikawa

I was born on 15 April 1955 in Toronto, Canada, and have lived in this city most of my life. I am a Sansei (third generation Japanese Canadian). My parents and grandparents were interned by the Canadian government during World War II. I have worked in community and women's organizations for the past fourteen years. I have a M.A. in sociology in education, specializing in feminist and anti-racist studies. I am one of the editors and contributors to "Awakening Thunder," issue 30 of *Fireweed*, a feminist quarterly. This special issue is the first published anthology of creative work by Asian Canadian women.

This is the first "erotic" story I have ever published. Its origins stem, in part, from a conversation I had with Tee Corinne about a story I'd written chronicling a safer sex workshop I'd attended at the first national Asian/Pacifica Lesbian Network retreat in 1989. The other parts come from my exploration and defining of my sexuality, for and by myself, after the end of an eight-year lesbian relationship. Issues concerning emotional and physical safety have been crucial to this self-definition. I have felt the need to read about other lesbians' experiences of doing safer sex, and thus decided to attempt it in my writing. This representation is not meant to be prescriptive, but rather is reflective of my own struggle at this point in herstory, given the limitations of my knowledge. In truth, I found writing about safer sex much easier than integrating it into my life. I am indebted to Merle Woo for her poem, "Untitled," in *The Forbidden Stitch* (Calyx, 1989). I would also like to thank Milagros Paredes and Rhonda Hackett for sharing their knowledge with me, and warm appreciation to Tee Corinne for her support and encouragement.

Concetta (Connie) Panzarino

I was born on 11/26/47 in Brooklyn, N.Y. I grew up in Brooklyn and then on Long Island in an Italian Catholic family. At 7 months old those around me became aware that I was severely disabled with a neuromuscular disease which left me brilliant, creative, sensuous, and unable to independently move most parts of my body. I was not allowed to go to grade school because there was no one to take responsibility to asist me to the toilet, so I had one hour per day of home instruction. Eventually I was mainstreamed into the public school system, achieved a B.A. in English from Hofstra University in 1969, and received my M.A. in Art Therapy from New York University in 1983. I have written numerous articles, short stories, and poems, and given lectures and workshops on ableism, homophobia, lesbianism, and feminism. I have also exhibited my artwork in shows and publications on a national level. Articles about me appear in *Eye to Eye, Portraits of Lesbians* by JEB, *Disabled, Female, and Proud*, by Harilyn Rousso (Exceptional Parent Press), and *Lesbian Land*, edited by Joyce Cheney.

Writing and talking about sexuality is revolutionary for all women, but especially for lesbians, and even more important for lesbians with disabilites who must fight the myth of asexuality in the lesbian community and in the world at large.

Vickie L. Sears (Cherokee/Spanish/English)

I was born 8/2/41 in San Diego, California, but was raised in Washington state. I have a Master of Social Work degree and am a member of the Academy of Certified Social Workers. I've been working as a therapist since 1968 and have taught workshops as well as course work at Pacific Lutheran and Western Washington State universities.

My poems, stories and articles have appeared in *Spider Woman's Granddaughters, Changing Our Power: An Introduction to Women's Studies, Feminist Perspectives of Ethics in Psychotherapy, Dancing on the Rim of the World, Sinister Wisdom, Ikon, Backbone, A Gathering of Spirit, The Things That Divide Us* and *Gathering Ground*. I received a writing grant from the Barbara Deming Memorial Fund for Women and a grant to go to The Cottages at Hedgebrook—a Women's Writing Colony. I was a short story contest winner in the 1990 Seattle Arts Commission competition. *Simple Songs: Stories by Vickie Sears* was nominated for a 1991 Lambda Literary Award.

My interest in writing stories about sex was not as great as it was to write a story about love and growing. Sex just happens to be a normal and joyous part of the sharing of love. I was seeking to talk about the difficulties of listening to each other while you build a friendship which may or may not turn into an affair or a long-term healthy relationship. I believe being sexual, however one defines it for themselves, can be a vital activity whatever your age or physical conditions. It's an aspect of living too seldom addressed. I wanted to do that, to illustrate that, as a part of Thelma and Maiselle's growing older together.

Sabrina Sojourner

Born October 23, 1952, Camp LeJuene, NC: 0.0 degrees Scorpio Sun; Libra Rising, Sagittarius Moon. I grew up in California, my family having moved there after my dad returned from the Korean War. We started in Oakland where my great-aunt and uncle lived, moved to San Francisco while my parents finished school, and made our way down the peninsula: Menlo Park, East Palo Alto, and San Jose. I graduated from Cupertino High School in 1970 and could not leave home fast enough. My first published piece of fiction appeared in *Intricate Passions*, Tee Corinne, ed., Banned Books, 1989. "From the House of Yemanja: The Goddess Heritage of Black Women" is in *The Politics of Women's Spirituality*, Charlene Spretnak, ed., Doubleday and Co., 1981. In January, 1991, I received the Pioneer Black Journalist Editorial Award from the Atlanta Association of Black Journalists for an essay, "Accepting Difference," printed in the July 1990 issue of *BLK Magazine*. I am the first "out" gay person to be honored by this group. At this writing I am preparing to move to Washington, DC.

I started writing stories in 1987 with the deliberate intent of making them sexual and lesbian-specific. During that time I was also writing a narrative about my recovery as an incest survivor. At the time I viewed writing erotica as a tool through which I could reclaim my sexuality. I continue to write sex stories because they are fun, challenging and healing. I believe women, perhaps particularly those of us who have been sexually abused, need to have examples of women enjoying—if not basking in—sexuality! We need more stories with female-centered perspectives which take the time to explore the range of what it means to be woman and lesbian.

Christina Springer

Christina Springer was born on June 23, 1964 at The Foundling Hospital in New York. Her parents (both native New Yorkers) decided raising children in New York was for the insane. She grew up in Pittsburgh, Pennsylvania, where she attended the Winchester-Thurston School For Girls (her first hint at the incredible bonds that can happen between women was there). She graduated from high school early to attend Antioch College where she received her B.A. with a triple concentration in Theater-Dance-Literature. She is a mother, a writer and a filmmaker. She co-founded a women's media collective, Back Porch Productions, with Casi Pacilio and L.M. Keys. The first film from the collective, "Out Of Our Time," has received international attention. Her screenplay, "Creation of Destiny," will be in production shortly. Springer's work has been seen in numerous periodicals including: *Shooting Star Review, Sojourner, Mothering Magazine, off our backs, New Directions For Women, Common Lives/Lesbian Lives, Woman of Power* and others. Her work is forthcoming in two anthologies by Terri Jewell and Stephanie Byrd.

Writing is a curious exercise. Writing erotica is an exercise of courage, balance, and exploration. I chose to begin writing erotica because I am an African-American and a mother. The marketplace for erotica by women demonstrated to me a distinct lack of reflection. The erotica

I had been reading lacked a depth common to my Black lesbian experience. It also most certainly did not include children.

Fantasy is a magical element. In fantasy we use our thoughts to conjure forth desire, thrill and ecstasy. As a mother, intimacy with my partner is a "catch as catch can" phenomena, usually occurring during school hours or after bed time. Fantasy, therefore, becomes a space where we invoke the memory of each other's deliciousness. More than that, however, our fantasies are guide posts on our journey to healing. Evaluation of our fantasies helps determine attitudes, beliefs and emotional responses to certain stimulus. Well used, fantasy lays the foundation for our progress as women healing from a racist patriarchy. To re-work fantasy gives a power to decide what is personally moving and exciting. Sex is more than a physical sensation. It is a spiritual, emotional and political journey encountered by self or across the seas of each other's souls. It is a distinct and dynamic part of our lives. Erotica, then, becomes a word for the documentation of wholeness.

Pearl Time'sChild

I have lived most of my life in the same west coast, semi-rural area where I was born. I have a doctorate, and teach college under another name. On October 22, 1990, I celebrated my 50th birthday by having my ears pierced for the first time, and getting earrings from my friends.

I wrote this story on pages I marked "Private! Do *not* share with *anyone!*" Promising myself that was the only way I could write it down at all; and I needed to talk to myself. But later, well, I have some very supportive friends who enjoy hearing what I write. So I took a chance, and things went from there to here.

It is now 8 years since the time of the story. So far I have not explored further the sexual realms I wrote about in "One August," for a number of reasons. . . . Since that time, Jo and I have been non-monogamous. It was very painful at first; for a while we weren't lovers. But now we have been again for many years. She is a grandmother these days and lives in another town. Soon we will be ten years friends-and-lovers: we plan to throw a party.

Chea Villanueva

I was born in 1952 in Philadelphia, Pennsylvania, to bi-racial parents. My father is Filipino (born in Luzon, Philippines), my mother Irish (from the United States). My parents were discriminated against because they married out of their own race. They were not well educated and my father worked as a cook and a machinist. They gave their children a lot of love and attention (there were four of us) but could not afford many material things. As a result I grew up in a poor working class city neighborhood.

My parents suffered lots of hardships. My brother died two weeks before my birth, my sisters married no-good men, and my mother died when I was ten years old. After she died I was left to fend for myself while my father worked and drank very hard. I became a classic juvenile delinquent and also loved girls during my pre-adolescent and teenage years. I spent a lot of my time in and out of homes for girls and reform schools. During the second week of tenth grade I quit school and got a menial factory job. I worked in a wax works that produced candles, a rug factory, a button company that produced plastic buttons, and a textile mill. At nineteen I decided to be a printer and got a job as an apprentice in a company that printed books and magazines. I went to school at night and got my GED and stayed in the printing business for 15 years.

At 38 years old my life is a lot different from back then. I went back to school and graduated with honors and am now employed as a Registered Medical Assistant. I am thinking of becoming a Doctor, but for now am studying related health sciences.

Because there is a part of me that will always be a rebel I like to write stories about my past and the events and people in my life that have made me what I am today. My work has been published in *Common Lives/Lesbian Lives*, *Making Waves* (an Asian Women's Anthology), *Feminary*, *Matrix*, *Big Apple Dyke News*, and *Ang Katipunan* (Union of Democratic Filipinos). I have written and had published a book of lesbian love poems, *The Things I Never Told You* and *Girlfriends*, a story about love, suspense, and *sex* between women!

Celeste West

I was born in the Chinese Year of the Horse, 1942, a wild and tender Sagittarian, with Mercury in Scorpio. So naturally, I not only love sex, but enjoy reading & writing about it. My first book on "S & S" (sex & spirituality), is called *Lesbian Love Advisor* (available from Booklegger Publishing, 555 29th Street, San Francisco 94131, $12, signed.) Soon I will have a 900 number as "Lesbian Love Advisor," which you can call if you want good phone. Tasteful, of course, just like they teach us at the Lesbian Finishing School in San Francisco, which I have attended for twenty years.

I am a scribe because it is a very good way to make very little money, and I don't have to pay war taxes. I have managed one magazine, written five books: *Revolting Librarians; Passionate Perils of Publishing; Elsa: I Come With My Songs*, with Elsa Gidlow; *Words In Our Pockets: The Feminist Writers Guild Handbook; Lesbian Love Advisor*. Part-time I also run the Library/Bookstore at the San Francisco Zen Center. The ultimate excitement for this sensualist is austere Zen minimalism ("From the withered tree, a blossom") — all enhanced by an emerging women's priesthood in Buddhism.

Along with diving into women's mysteries, I am living in "menamorphosis," changing from Artemis to Aphrodite with downright cheer. I receive the silver-rose incandescence in "Proud Mary" perhaps because I have *petite mal*, perhaps because I like LSD, perhaps because my electromagnetic chemical force fields have been so galvanized over the years by certain sterling Lesbians. Oh, the Lesbian bodies electric . . .

Although I was trained as a freelance journalist, I sometimes now play with fiction. I received a sign when the women's bookstores kept putting *Lesbian Love Advisor* in the "Fiction" and "Humor" sections. Something my woman journalism teacher once said also flashed back to me: "If you want to write fiction, be a journalist, if you want to write truth be a novelist." Besides, if I don't clothe my juciful, paradoxical Lesbian sex as fiction, I'll be sued or worse.

My forthcoming book is called *The Passionate Pearls of Pluralism & Other Lesbian Conundrums*. It is a novel·ty for the polyfidelious Lesbian-About-Town, full of hand jive, heavy vanilla, even "Tips for Tops," such as, "What is the very first thing I should do when I go to bed with a woman?" Answer: "Take off your ankle weights." See you at the gym.

zana

born 3/7/47, new jersey. also lived in baltimore, then texas, where i graduated high school. worked clerical jobs, finally wangled a journalism position, doing my own writing and art on the side. my work has appeared in many lesbian/feminist periodicals and anthologies during the past 11 years. i've also published a collection of my poetry and drawings, *herb womon*, available for $7 from me at 12150 w. calle seneca, tucson, az 85743.

a friend of mine says her dyke community tries to share details of their sex practices just as they talk about other aspects of daily life. i want to do that, too— i think secrecy about sex keeps us from really knowing each other, and from developing our full, true, lesbian sexualities. erotic writing has not come easily for me. i've wanted to avoid the predictable descriptions that make most erotica *un*exciting (to me); yet it's hard to find words for what is, essentially, beyond words. i wrote "september" after the relationship's end. i was greatly missing being sexual with her. writing about how it had been allowed me to relive it briefly— i loved being in those moments one more time!

Banned Books titles from Tee Corinne

Authored by Tee Corinne

Dreams of the Woman Who Loved Sex $7.95

Lovers: Love and Sex Stories $7.95

Edited by Tee Corinne

Intricate Passions $8.95

Riding Desire $9.95

Available from your favorite bookseller or by mail from Banned Books. Send a first-class postage stamp for our free catalog of titles and a list of bookstores.

Banned Books
#292, P.O. Box 33280
Austin, Texas 78764

Add $1.50 postage and handling. Texas residents, please add 8% sales tax.